TRAIL OF MONSTERS

TRAIL OF MONSTERS

by

C.E. Osborn

This is a work of fiction. Names, characters, businesses, places, events and incidents are either the products of the author's imagination or used in a fictitious manner. Any resemblance to actual persons, living or dead, or actual events is purely coincidental.

Cover design:
SelfPubBookCovers.com/RLSather

© 2021
C.E. Osborn
All rights reserved

For Bill and Marsha H.

CHAPTER 1

"What are you going to do while I'm gone?" Autumn Hunter asked as she tossed a pair of jeans into a suitcase.

"I was thinking I might head down to Oregon and visit Brandon. Maybe while I'm there, I can get started on the book," Zach Larson replied.

Autumn nodded and added some shirts to the bag. She was getting ready to attend a library conference in Chicago. He had finished filming several episodes of the reality television show *Creature Hunt* and had been excited to spend some time with his girlfriend. She had told him about the conference when he had returned home last night. While he was unhappy about only spending a couple of days with her, he knew he could find some interesting things to do while she was gone.

They had moved in together a few months ago, after Zach had decided to buy a house at the edge of town with plenty of room for both of them to have a space for relaxation and research. Autumn's cat, Squatch, had not taken long to claim certain places throughout the house, and one of those areas was the recliner in Zach's office. He had tried to bring the cat over to Autumn's reading room a few times, but the cat always came back into the office and meowed at him before once again settling on the chair.

Zach had been happy that, for the first time since starting his job as the host of the show, he hadn't had to hire someone to come in and check on the house while he was away. Autumn, still getting used to sharing her private space with him, had both missed him and enjoyed her time alone. Now, they were once again going to be apart.

Autumn seemed to read his mind. "It's only for a week. After I get back, we'll have a few months before you start filming again."

He hugged her. "I know."

She closed the zipper on her bag. "Let me finish up here, then I'll check on what we have for dinner."

"I'll go call Brandon."

"Great."

Zach went down to his office. The cat followed Autumn as she went into the bathroom to gather up some personal items for the trip. He sat down at his desk and called his cameraman and good friend Brandon Taylor. They had just seen each other a couple of days ago at an airport in New Orleans, when each of them had boarded flights to separate cities. Zach had flown back to Seattle, while Brandon had flown into Portland and driven back to his home in Albany, Oregon.

Brandon answered with a relaxed tone in his voice. "Hey, Zach. What's up?"

"Hey, Brandon. I'm going to be heading down in your direction for about a week. Are you going to be home?"

"Sorry, Zach. I promised my lady I'd take her on a real vacation."

"Where are you going?"

"Hawaii. Hold on a second." Zach heard Brandon speaking to someone in the background. "Okay. You know I just moved to Albany last year, but people like to talk to me when they learn I'm involved with the show. Even if I won't be here, I can point you in the direction of some weird crap."

"That's exactly what I'm looking for."

"This area has a lot of wineries and campgrounds. There are large forests around here, too. I've been hearing some stories about people camping down here and seeing and hearing large creatures move through the trees and bushes. One campground, in particular, would be worth checking out on your way down here. I think it's called Shadow Point. There are claims that the devil lives there in the form of a goat. One couple was on the local news last night claiming they saw Bigfoot and what sounded like maybe some sort of dogman at a winery that actually celebrates a lot of those things."

"The dogman in Oregon? That's the first time I've heard about that. Is it supposed to be the same type of creature that we investigated in Wisconsin and Minnesota?"

"Sounds like it."

Zach started making notes. "Thanks, Brandon."

"Tasha works part-time at one of the wineries and said she hears something behind the tasting room now and then when she stays late. She's been afraid to walk to her car by herself and one of her co-workers always goes with her."

"Which winery is that?"

"Old Forest Cellars. It's just outside the town of Vineville, along with some other popular wineries. Hold on a minute." Brandon spoke to someone in the background, and then Zach heard Tasha say "Hi, Zach."

"Hi, Tasha. Hope you enjoy Hawaii."

"Thanks. I just wanted to let you know that Old Forest is having a music and arts festival this coming weekend, from Thursday to Sunday. A lot of people will be camping at the winery, and there are a few small cabins available for rent."

"At a winery?"

"Yep. That's how they make some extra money during the winter, by offering people a place to stay while they go on off-season tours of wine country."

"Do you think all the cabins are full?"

"I know there was at least one empty one still available. It's small, and has a bed, a bathroom, and a microwave and refrigerator. I'll call the owner, Nancy Dakota, and let her know that you'll be calling about it."

"Thanks. I'm planning to arrive in the Albany area on Wednesday."

"Awesome." Tasha's voice dropped. "That thing I've been hearing behind the winery?"

"Yes?"

"The one time that I turned around to look for it I thought I saw something sticking up from its head. Ears, or horns." She laughed uneasily. "Maybe just my imagination. Too many stories from Brandon."

Zach's heart started racing as he made some notes on the page in front of him. "Probably."

"Have a good trip, Zach." She handed the phone back to Brandon.

"You get everything?"

"I think so. Thanks, Brandon. I'll call Old Forest right after this."

"Didn't you get enough adventure in the last four months?"

Zach thought back to their recent investigations. Although interesting, the producers had seemed to focus a lot more on supernatural and spiritual beings, including vampires and ghosts. Their last episode, filmed in New Orleans, had been about vampires, and Zach had felt uneasy while speaking to several witnesses. He preferred to be searching for possible flesh and blood creatures like Bigfoot, but he knew that the show had always been driven to investigate all aspects of the paranormal. The producers had promised a return to something more in his field of interest when the show resumed filming in September.

However, this was June, and he had a purpose for the trip. "Autumn and I decided last year to write a book about cryptids in the Pacific Northwest. We're including Washington, Oregon, and some parts of British Columbia. She started a couple of chapters while I was away for the show. She's leaving for a library conference tomorrow and I'm going to set out on my own investigation. I've heard a few other stories about creepy stuff down in Oregon, and it's close enough for a road trip."

"On your way down here, stop by Mount Saint Helens," Brandon advised.

"Why?"

"Have you heard of the Batsquatch?"

Zach was surprised into laughter. "No, that one has eluded me."

"Look it up. Hey, Tasha's asking me to finish packing. Good luck, Zach."

"Bye, Brandon. Have a good trip."

Zach looked up the Batsquatch online. He opened a new

notebook and copied down some information about the creature he saw on the screen. He added Bigfoot, listed some possible goatman sightings after finding the campground Brandon had told him about, and even added the dogman and the ever-present term of "other creatures" to the list. Satisfied, he set the notebook in the middle of the desk and looked up wineries and campgrounds near Albany.

He found the website for Old Forest Cellars. It appeared to be one of three wineries that bordered a wilderness area simply labeled as Old Forest. Zach saw that six cabins were listed as being an option for rent, although they were shown as unavailable when he put in the dates of his upcoming stay. Another look at the layout of the cabins showed a seventh, smaller building set away from the others. He nodded and dialed the number listed on the website. A woman, sounding tired and busy, answered the phone. "Old Forest Cellars, Nancy speaking."

"Hi, Nancy. My name is Zach Larson. One of your employees, Tasha Taylor, said she was going to call you about letting me stay in a cabin this weekend."

"Oh, yes!" Nancy's voice perked up. "Zach. She didn't mention your last name. Are you the guy from that show *Creature Hunt*?"

"Yes, that's me."

"Good. Maybe you can come down and figure out what's scaring people around here."

"I'm certainly interested in whatever I can find."

"I do have the one cabin left. Tasha said she described it to you and you were still interested."

"I've stayed in worse places."

"I bet you have." She chuckled. "Okay. I've made a note that you'll probably arrive on Wednesday and I'll keep the cabin for you until Sunday. When you get here, just ask for me and whoever's around will come and find me.

"Perfect. Thank you, Nancy."

"Looking forward to meeting you, Zach."

He hung up the phone and found a website for the town of

Vineville. The map showed a downtown area with several businesses, a medical clinic, a couple of schools, and some other commercial properties. Old Forest Cellars was listed as being an area attraction, as well as a place called Grape Valley and the curiously named Legends Vineyard. He booked a site at the Saint Helens Campground and decided to take a chance on sleeping wherever he could between Portland and Albany Tuesday night before heading deeper into Oregon. He started making a list of what he would need to bring with him.

"Zach?" He turned and saw Autumn at the office door. "I didn't find anything good in the kitchen. Let's go out."

"Sure," he agreed. He turned off the computer and headed down the hall with Autumn. He was curious about what he would find during his week-long investigation and was really looking forward to the adventure.

CHAPTER 2

The next morning, Monday, Zach and Autumn both made final preparations for their trips. While Autumn was in the shower, Zach went out to his truck and placed his backpack behind the passenger seat. He made sure there was room for Autumn's bags in the back of the cab, then closed the door. He smiled at the truck. It had been a birthday present to himself in January, and had been specially ordered and outfitted for going on overnight camping trips.

He wandered to the back of the dark gray truck, unlatched the upper window of the black canopy, and opened the tailgate. The canopy had windows on the two longer sides with attached screens so they could be opened for air during the night. The back window locked tightly from inside, and all of the windows had dark curtains that could be tied off to the side during the day.

The bed of the truck had a layer of padding covered by a thin gray carpet. Zach moved to the garage and brought out a sleeping bag and some pillows. One of the equipment boxes tucked up by the cab already had some blankets inside, along with other camping equipment. Another container was freshly packed with snacks, and Zach had filled a small cooler with ice packs and drinks this morning. He'd refill the cooler as needed during the trip. He had everything necessary to simply pull into a campground, get out, get himself settled in back, and sleep comfortably. He could also observe his surroundings from the back of the truck if something disturbed him in the middle of the night.

He climbed into the truck bed and opened the padlock on a smaller box tucked off to the side of the equipment box. He had placed a few cans of bear spray inside, as well as the large knife that he now always carried on investigations like this. Physical encounters with Bigfoot and dogmen had taught him to be a little more proactive in self-defense. On the show, he didn't worry as much because they had an armed security guard following the crew.

He closed and locked the tailgate and window, assured that everything was there. He went back into the house and found Autumn just closing the door of the cat carrier. "Oh, you should have asked me to help," he said with a wink.

"Yes, because Squatch just loves it when you put him in here?" she responded with a laugh. The cat liked to hang out with Zach, but the last time Zach had tried to take him to the vet he had ended up with a bandaged arm.

"Let's get going. After I drop you off, I'm driving directly down to one of the campsites near Mount Saint Helens."

"I still think that Batsquatch is something Brandon made up," Autumn said.

"The great believer in cryptids is dismissive of a creature because she's never heard about it before?" Zach asked. "There was even an article in this city's newspaper about it."

"Okay, people have seen something. But a flying Bigfoot?" Autumn shook her head. "Well, you're only staying there for one night, right? Chances are slim that you'll see anything."

"Famous last words," Zach laughed.

"Why don't you stop at a lake on your trip and see if you can spot some slithery eel-looking creature?" Autumn asked, then laughed when Zach rolled his eyes. She knew about his aversion to underwater creatures, even those animals that were well-documented and common to bodies of water.

They locked the house and drove to the vet. Autumn went inside and made sure Squatch got settled into the boarding room. They headed to the airport, where Zach maneuvered the truck through traffic until he reached the drop-off lanes for the airline Autumn was flying to Chicago.

"I'll call when I get there," she said after he had retrieved her bags from the truck. "You're driving straight down to the campground?"

"With a few scenic stops," he said. He kissed her. "Have a good time. Do some exploring."

"We'll see," she replied. She waved as one of her co-workers came into view. "Bye, Zach."

"Bye, Autumn."

He waited until she was inside the airport, then hurried back to the truck and found a way out of the departure lanes. Ten minutes later, he was on the freeway heading south to Mount Saint Helens.

He stopped once for a quick lunch. It was early afternoon by the time he reached the end of the mountain highway and paid an entrance fee at the visitor center. He had passed the campground on the way into the park and it had already seemed crowded, so although he had a reservation he decided to not linger too long at the center.

Zach wandered in and checked out the displays of the famous eruption and the path of the mudflow that had caused much of the devastation in the area. He watched a movie of the eruption, then looked through the gift shop. A few items looked interesting, and he finally decided to buy a book of the history surrounding the eruption and the impacts on the animals and nature throughout the region.

He wandered outside and over to the stone fence that kept people from accidentally going over the edge of the cliff. He marveled at the tracks of mudflow destruction that could still be seen on the landscape. There had been lots of people, and animals, that had lost their lives in the eruption. He remembered seeing footage of animals fleeing from the forests, and wondered if there had been any Bigfoot seen in the area.

He returned to his truck and drove back down the highway. When he reached the entrance to the Saint Helens Campground, he turned in and parked the truck in front of the office. There were spots for RVs, a few basic cabins, and lots of sites for tent camping. He was third in line at the check-in desk. When he finally stepped forward to speak to the woman behind the counter, he was the only guest remaining in the office.

"Hi, I'm Kathy Morelli," she greeted him. "May I have your name?"

"Zach Larson."

She looked at her computer screen. "Oh, yes. You made your reservation last night. We have two possible sites for you. One is a tent site at the very end of a row of RV sites, very close to the bathrooms. The other is the RV site right next to it."

"I'll take the tent site. I assume it's okay if I just sleep in my truck?"

"Whatever makes you comfortable," she said. A man came into the office from a doorway that connected to the general store next door. "This is my husband, Blair. I'm giving Zach here the last tent site."

Blair slipped behind the counter and placed a paper map of the campground on the counter. He circled Zach's site. "It's down this lane, at the very end."

"Thanks." Zach handed over his credit card and decided to jump right in. "Have either of you ever heard about someone seeing monsters around the mountain?"

"What, like Bigfoot?" Kathy asked. "My uncle once claimed he saw one, but it turned out to be something else."

"What about flying creatures?" For some reason, Zach found himself shying away from actually saying the word Batsquatch out loud.

"Only bats and birds," Blair said. He smiled at him. "And no one's ever said they've seen a Bigfoot wandering around the campground."

"Good thing, too," Kathy said. "We don't need any of that weirdness here."

Zach smiled. He took his card back and they explained a few of the rules to him. "General store is open until ten. There are lots of restaurants just a few miles away if you don't want to cook at your site. Front gates are open all night," Blair said.

"Thank you," Zach said. He left the office and drove to his site. It was well-marked, with a water spigot at the end of a cement parking pad and a picnic table. He unloaded two chairs and a battery-powered lantern, then found a wood pile and brought a few logs back to his site. He pulled a bottle of water out of the cooler and sat down to start reading his new book.

A couple of hours later, he put it down with some reluctance. One picture in particular had caught his attention. He didn't know if the photographer had even noticed, but there was a massive shape in the background of a photo of a house that had been carried by the mud flow and had come to rest against a grove of trees.

Zach looked at the picture again. Surely someone had commented on the large figure just beyond the trees, but there was nothing in the caption about it, and no mention of it in the surrounding paragraphs. He flipped forward through the book until he found a chapter that contained several unverified stories. One such story included a man's account of several large ape-like creatures supposedly communicating with first responders in the area after the eruption. The author glossed over the story, but Zach wondered if there was some truth to it. He decided to take a chance on talking to either Blair or Kathy again before he left.

He realized he was hungry. While he had been reading, a large RV had pulled into the empty site two spots away from him and they had started cooking something that smelled wonderful. He left the chairs and lantern on the table and got back into his truck. He'd find dinner somewhere along the road and then come back to continue his research.

CHAPTER 3

Zach returned from dinner and found his campsite again. The sun was starting to set, so he turned on a lantern and built a fire. As he added another log to it, he saw Blair walking down the road with a large flashlight in his hand. The flashlight was off, but Zach assumed he had brought it in case he was still making rounds after dark. He waved, and Blair walked over to the fire pit.

"Hello there. Getting settled in for the evening?"

"Yep." Zach heard kids shouting from the closest RV. "This place is busy tonight."

"Like Kathy told you, this was the last empty tent site and the one next to you is the only empty RV site. School is out, so parents are traveling with their kids."

"Please have a seat." Zach motioned to the other chair. "And help yourself to anything in the cooler."

"Thanks." Blair sent a brief message to Kathy over the radio. He pulled out a soda and twisted the cap off the bottle, then drank nearly half of it before setting it down on the table. "Kathy recognized your name and said you look for weird things on television."

Zach laughed. "I guess that's a good way to think of it." He described the show to Blair. "I'm going to be direct here. Have you ever heard of a Batsquatch?"

Blair looked at the fire and rubbed a finger against his soda bottle. "Heard of it, yes. There are stories going back decades about something big hiding in the trees around here. Right after the eruption, sightings seemed to spike. I always assumed they were talking about the typical Bigfoot, but some of them included creatures that seemed to soar from tree to tree."

Zach thought about the eruption of Mount Saint Helens forty years ago. He had not been born yet, but like most kids growing up in the state he had learned about in local history and science classes. "I imagine people were thinking they saw all sorts of strange animals back then."

"Yep. Most were probably normal animals forced into new habitats and acting strangely. Kathy mentioned her uncle. He claimed there was a Bigfoot walking in the trees beyond his yard, and that it was glancing around like it was looking for something. When Kathy's father was called to come over and look at it, it turned out to be a bear on its hind legs rubbing its face against the tree." Blair shook his head. "Lots of stories ended that way back then."

They turned as a family walked past the site. Blair waved, and the parents nodded in return while the kids concentrated on keeping their bikes straight in the road. "I don't think this campground would be quiet enough for something like a Batsquatch to hunt for whatever it needs."

"If it's anything like a bear or other large animals, the smell of food might attract it," Zach pointed out. "I'll probably stay up late tonight to see if anything appears."

Blair stood and finished his soda. "Quiet hours start at ten," he reminded Zach with a smile. "Hope your night goes well." He took his bottle with him as he walked away, then threw it into the recycling bin on his way to check on the bathrooms.

Zach wondered if Blair knew more than he had let on. He shrugged and put another log on the fire. Around him, people at other sites were gathered around fires and picnic tables, laughing and talking and playing games. He sat back and stared off into the forest. Now and then a pair of eyes showed up and were reflected in the light, but a deer always emerged, looked around, and ran back into the trees.

Around nine-thirty, Zach went to the bathroom. On his way back, he noticed that most sites had quieted down. Any people still outside were talking softly. He double-checked the fire pit to make sure the embers were no longer glowing, then climbed into the back of the truck. He closed the curtains and changed into flannel pants and a t-shirt, then opened the windows. He kept the curtains closed.

He made some notes by lantern light, then put away the notebook. He turned off all the lights, felt around to be sure at least one weapon was in reach if he needed it during the night, and laid down in his sleeping bag, pulling a blanket over him.

The moon was almost full, and he could see its light at the edge of the curtains. He waited for the campground to fall silent, and for a time all he could hear were the usual insect noises and animal calls in the forest. Occasionally he did hear people talking as they passed the site to walk to the bathroom. He sat up a couple of times and moved the curtains to look out, but didn't see anything unusual.

Around twelve-thirty, he decided to go to sleep. As he closed his eyes, he realized that most of the natural noises had stopped. He heard a loud thump behind the campsite that was followed by a rustling in the bushes. It wasn't the sound of wood hitting wood that he would have expected if a Bigfoot was in the area. It sounded like flesh hitting a tree. He moved to the back window with his phone in his hand and looked out.

An animal lay on the ground, apparently dead. It was small, but Zach took a picture of it anyway. He thought it was a raccoon, and when he moved slightly to get a better angle that was confirmed. He wondered what had killed it. He waited, but no further movement came from the brush.

Zach let the curtain fall and quietly laid down. His heart had started racing, but he took a few deep breaths and calmed down. Maybe in the morning he'd be able to find some sort of evidence that would point to whatever had just found its next meal. He closed his eyes and heard the insects chirping. Whatever dangerous animal was out there before had now gone away. He fell into a sound sleep, dreaming of shadows crossing a gravel road.

When he woke up the next morning to bright light underneath the curtains, he yawned and blinked from the bright sunlight streaming in underneath the curtains. He remembered where he was and sat up. Looking out the window, he saw that the raccoon was still there. Ignoring his body's desire to lay back down, he climbed out of the truck and walked over to the dead animal.

It was intact, except for the large dent in its head. He heard voices coming from a nearby site and kicked the raccoon under some bushes. He didn't want any kids to walk through here and pick up the raccoon. He didn't see any immediate sign of rabies, but it was still better to be safe.

He waved at the family in the RV, then stopped back at the truck to get some new clothes and his toiletries. The bathrooms were open with only a couple of other people inside, so he showered and shaved, feeling refreshed by putting on a clean shirt and jeans. He returned to the campsite and put everything back in his truck, then walked over to the store.

The campground served a small breakfast buffet and there was a seating area beyond the store that he hadn't seen last night. He waved at Kathy and Blair as he gathered his food, then found a table for two in the corner. Kathy came over to him and sat down across from him.

"Where are you headed next?" she asked in a low, pleasant voice.

"I'm not sure where I'm staying tonight. Are there any places you would recommend?"

"Are you sure you want to go looking for monsters?"

"Absolutely."

She motioned for Blair to come over. "Honey, take this seat while I cover the front desk. Why don't you tell Zach about Shadow Point?"

Blair sat down in her place. "Any signs of a Batsquatch last night?"

"No," Zach replied honestly. There had been something out in the woods, but he had not seen anything that would point to a flying ape-like creature.

"I thought so." Blair shook his head. "About a year ago, someone in our group of campground managers disappeared. He was living on site at a place down in Oregon called Shadow Point. It's a few hours down the interstate and off to the east."

'That sounds familiar." Zach pulled out his phone and opened the memo section, reading quickly. "I think one of my co-workers mentioned that place to me. Yes. Shadow Point." Blair repeated the address for confirmation. "Have you been there yourself?"

"Just once. We all try to stay at each other's sites so we would know what to recommend to our guests. Business can be slow between October and April, so it's nice when people refer to us when travelers are asking for a place to camp."

"What happened to the manager?"

"Bill Taylor just disappeared one night. As I understand from other people in our group discussing it, his house was ransacked and the police found signs of an animal outside." Blair shook his head. "He was a really nice guy, but even in daylight Shadow Point always felt like its name. Like the sun was hardly ever able to get all the way down in there. That's how dense the forest is at that campground."

Zach nodded. He had been in a few areas that sounded similar, where there was always a sense of unease. Not being able to clearly see the sun often made people feel unsettled. "Are you telling me I should stay there tonight?"

"Stay there? That's up to you. But you should at least drive down there and look around. It's been a year, but maybe you'll see something the police didn't notice."

"Thanks." Zach put his phone away and Blair got up to talk to some other guests. He finished his breakfast and walked back to the campsite. When he arrived, he typed the address of Shadow Point into his navigation system. It was worth a look.

He stretched and decided it was time to leave. He stopped at the store to check out and bought a soda, then got back into his truck. Before getting back on the freeway, he drove down a scenic highway, pulling into overlooks and occasionally walking several feet into the forest. He saw and heard nothing. By the time he finally reached the interstate, it was already early afternoon.

CHAPTER 4

A few hours later, Zach realized he was lost. He had taken the correct freeway exit, but after that he couldn't remember where he was supposed to turn. The navigation screen didn't seem to be able to locate the precise location of the campground. He was annoyed and frustrated when he finally pulled into the parking lot of a small diner.

When he walked inside, he got an eerie feeling. He looked around and saw two men in dark suits, grim expressions on their faces, looking down at a piece of paper on their table and mumbling to each other. He also saw about ten other customers with menus or food in front of them. A sixties doo-wop song was playing, and a waitress in a blue dress with a white apron over it approached him.

"Table for one?" she asked in a friendly voice. Zach looked at his watch and shrugged.

"Sure," he said. It was already after six, and he hadn't realized until now that he was actually quite hungry. She led him to a booth near the window. "Is the Shadow Point Campground around here?" he asked as she placed the menu in front of him.

"A lot of people ask about that place," the waitress said. "My boss can tell you about it. Anything to drink?"

"Coffee, please," he said. He sat back and looked at the menu. As he did, he sensed eyes on him. He casually glanced around. No one seemed to be looking his way. He shook his head slightly. *Stop creeping yourself out*, he thought.

It wasn't even dark outside, but with the sun starting to go down in an hour or so Zach knew he should get back on the road as soon as possible. The waitress came back and he ordered a hamburger with fries. She nodded and left. Zach saw her say something to a man in slacks and a short-sleeve button-down shirt, who had had just emerged from an office behind the register. He looked over at Zach and nodded at the waitress, then walked over to Zach's booth.

"I'm the owner, Martin Cooper. Jean said you were asking

about the Shadow Point Campground?"

A bell rang over the door. Zach turned to see the two men in suits leaving the diner. He suddenly felt relaxed, as if a heavy weight had been lifted from the room. Martin sensed it as well. He frowned at the retreating men. "Mind if I join you?" he asked.

"Please." Martin slid into the booth across from Zach. "I heard about the campground from a couple of people I met yesterday. They said it was just off the highway, but I haven't been able to locate it."

"Shadow Point is just barely still a camping area, and not on very many maps. It's about twenty miles down the road, but no one maintains it anymore. The former manager, a middle-aged man named Bill Taylor, disappeared."

"Disappeared?" That fit Blair and Kathy's story.

"Yes. One morning two campers went by his house to check out. They found the door open and hoof prints in the dirt around the porch. There were signs of a struggle inside, and a lot of blood outside in a trail that ended at the edge of the forest. The campers contacted the police."

"Did the police find anything?"

"No. And the hoof prints were the most confusing part. No one around there keeps horses or pigs, and they couldn't match the prints to either of those animals, anyway."

Zach's meal arrived, and Jean also set down a soda for Martin and water for Zach. "Thank you," he said to her, his mind wandering. He took a bite of his hamburger. It was delicious.

"Anyway, ever since then it's been listed as available for camping, and often attracts people who are on hiking trips or people driving through who just need a place to pull over and sleep for the night without being bothered by a lot of people around. It's owned by a local auto mechanic. He just lets people come and go at the site and has a company come in and clean the bathrooms. Otherwise, everyone is on their own." Martin took a sip of his soda. "Those guys who just left? They go over there once or twice a month. Some of the people who camp at Shadow Point stop here for breakfast on their way to the interstate. They've told me that those guys sit in a car near the manager's cabin all night and hardly ever get out or speak to anyone. That started just after Bill went missing."

"Some sort of security, maybe?"

"Doubtful. More like they're looking for something." Martin shook his head. "You couldn't pay me enough to stay out there."

"Sounds like an interesting place. Maybe I should keep going and see what's out there." Zach looked down and realized that his plate was almost empty.

"Do yourself a favor and head back to the freeway. There's a nice hotel, the Oregon Inn, run by my brother. Tell him I sent you, and he'll give you a good rate. It'll be better, and safer, than Shadow Point."

Zach finished his coffee. "I think I'll drive down to the campground. If I feel it's going to be dangerous, I'll head to that hotel."

"I'll wave when you drive by later," Martin promised. He returned to his office and Jean came back to the table.

"Anything else?" she asked with a smile.

Zach looked at the dessert menu on the table. "Just a piece of the chocolate cream pie."

"No problem." She removed his plate and refilled his coffee. He pulled out his phone and looked up the Shadow Point Campground again. Brandon had mentioned it, but Kathy and Blair's story had really gotten him interested, and now he was wondering if he could be in danger.

He was able to find a few reviews about the place. The older ones, from before the manager had gone missing, were mostly five stars, claiming it was cheap and a good place to set up a tent. In the last year, ratings had declined down to one star, with warnings of being disturbed by a stalker during the night or feeling watched in the creepy atmosphere. He decided to take a chance and drive out there. He had the equipment to defend himself, and since he had already driven all the way out here it seemed a shame to turn back now.

He finished the pie and paid, leaving Jean a generous tip. Martin was on the phone when he waved goodbye, and Zach guessed he was calling his brother to tell him to keep a room open for a possible guest later. He got back into his truck and turned right out of the parking lot. That would take him in the direction of Shadow Point.

He found the entrance almost exactly twenty miles later. There was an open gate off the highway and a sign that was clearly marked, but Zach still felt uneasy as he drove through the entrance. He reached a parking lot, and saw the former manager's house.

He got out, bringing a flashlight and his backpack with him. "Hello?" he called out as he knocked on the front door. The house was a large one-story log cabin, and the front door was unlocked when he tried the knob. "Is anyone here?" he asked. He stepped inside. His footsteps were loud on the wood floor.

The house was silent. Zach took a couple of minutes to look around. It looked like most of the personal belongings had been removed, but furniture was covered with dust and a rug in the living room had a faded blood stain right in the center of it. Zach pulled out his pocket knife and, seeing that a square had already been cut out by the police, took another one and placed it in a plastic bag. He looked around the corner of the living room into the kitchen and saw that someone had knocked out the glass in the back door and a window over the sink. He returned to the living room and walked down a short hallway that led to a bedroom, a bathroom, and a small office.

All of the other rooms had blood in them. Not one large stain like in the living room, but splatters on the walls and floors. Looking at the amount of blood, Zach realized that more than one person had probably been wounded or killed here by something with a strong blade, or strong claws and teeth.

He took pictures. Inside the bedroom, he walked over to

the nightstand and found a silver cross on it. "Tell them it's back," was written on a pad of paper. Zach wondered if Bill had written the note to himself before being attacked.

No creatures seemed to be hiding inside, but it was nearly dark and he no longer felt comfortable here. He left the house and closed the door. The front porch was covered by an overhang, which protected those standing on it and within a few feet around it from rain, snow, or sun. He studied the ground and was surprised to see hoof prints that were clear and defined.

"Those can't be from a year ago," he muttered. He took pictures of them, but he had no materials to do any casting. He noted the location of the prints in his notebook, and would fill in the rest of the story later.

"Time to look at the campsites," he said.

"Time," he heard someone echo behind him.

He turned around, aiming his flashlight at the bushes. Nothing appeared. "Who's there?" he asked, almost shouting.

No answer came. The bushes rustled beside the house, as if something or someone was heading his way. Zach's heart started racing, and he ran back into the house and shut the door behind him.

A loud laugh rang out, and Zach could hear it clearly through the open windows in the kitchen. He cursed as heavy steps walked around the side of the building and stopped at the front door. Zach, already halfway across the living room, realized he had not locked the door and slid around the wall that separated the kitchen from the front room. He tried to keep his breathing quiet as something shoved the front door open.

Zach waited. He heard heavy breathing, then the clicking sound of hooves on the wood floor briefly muted by the rug. He took a chance. "Hello?" he asked.

A moment passed. "Who are you?" he asked.

"Are you," the voice replied. Zach's brain tried to process the fact that the monster seemed to be repeating him.

"Did you kill someone here?"

"Kill."

A sharp blade sliced into the wall above Zach's head. He cried out in surprise and ran for the back door. He looked behind him and almost bruised his side with the doorknob as he threw the door open, panicking and desperate to get away from what he saw when he turned around.

It was tall, with goat-like legs, complete with hooves, and a broad chest. It had the head and face of a goat but human-like hands that carried a double-bladed ax. Horns grew from the top of its head and curled around, creating what Zach assumed must be a formidable weapon if the monster chose to use them. When it opened its mouth, he saw rows of sharp teeth, and the gleam in its very human and intelligent eyes made him pause.

"Kill," the goatman said, and Zach could still not believe that it was speaking to him. The words seemed like they barely fit with the movement of the monster's mouth.

He propelled himself through the door, tripped on the back steps, and rolled on the ground. After checking to make sure he wasn't hurt, he saw the creature standing at the door holding up the ax and grinning. He shuddered and ran around the side of the house, then finally reached his truck and got in, pounding the door lock button a few times.

When he was able to breathe normally again, he decided to see if the creature was still around, watching him. He turned on the headlights and some of the ferns near the house started shaking, indicating that something was walking through them. A deer emerged, and for a moment Zach had himself convinced that the goatman was trying to trick him.

"Calm down, calm down," he told himself. He waited, but nothing else emerged from the forest. A sense of safety, perhaps premature, began to flow through him. He decided to drive further into the campground and see if there was anything else there before he left. He was not staying here tonight.

He started the truck and drove down the gravel road. About half a mile into the campground, he found a building housing the bathrooms with four doors along the side, along with paths that led to four distinct clearings for tents and cars. He parked on one of the paths and got out, this time taking his flashlight and bear spray. Even against just another human, it would buy him enough time to get away.

He walked down the path ahead of him and found an empty clearing. He took some pictures of it, then backtracked to the restrooms. The power worked. He stepped inside the first door and was surprised to see a powerful bolt on the inside, along with a chain to connect the door to a bolt on the wall. "Someone was scared in here," he said, and took pictures. The other doors also all had similar locks. The bathrooms looked clean and functional, so he used one, washed his hands, then turned off the light and waited a minute before going back outside.

He walked down the path across from the truck and saw two tents set up in the clearing. "Hello?" he called. "My name is Zach. I'm just going to be looking around."

"Zach," a voice replied. He realized that it was the goatman again, apparently having come here after he left the house. The voice was low and had a growl-like tone to it.

"Anyone here?" he asked again, more quietly. No response came from the tents. The rest of the site was empty. Zach studied the tents from where he was, shining at them with his flashlight. One of them, on the other side of the clearing, was partially open and appeared to have a sleeping bag inside. Zach thought about walking over to the nearest tent, but he didn't want to scare anyone if they were hiding inside. Instead, he turned around and walked back out to his truck.

He stopped when he saw the truck. The two guys from the diner were there, standing just outside the glow from the headlights. They looked like government agents, and he started to wonder if they were here doing some sort of investigation. "Leave," one of them said in a flat voice.

"What happens if I stay?" he challenged them.

"Nothing good," the other guy said. "You're looking for

it, aren't you?"

"What do you think I'm looking for?"

"The thing that killed Bill Taylor."

Zach shook his head. "I didn't know what I'd find here."

"We'll be watching you."

"I'm going to leave now," Zach decided. "Once I'm gone, you can stop watching me."

"It might follow you," one of them warned. They stepped away from the vehicle and walked closer to the cement building.

"Follow," the low voice said from behind them. The men looked at each other, alarm on their faces. Zach turned, but once again saw nothing. He quickly brought up his camera and snapped a couple of pictures of the men. They rushed back into their car and drove away, apparently frightened by what they had heard. He climbed into the truck and drove down the road. He really wanted to be far away from Shadow Point.

He had just turned back onto the highway when he saw a car full of teenagers turning at the Shadow Point sign. He pulled off to the side of the road and contemplated following them. *Maybe the goatman was just after me for entering the house and those kids will be fine*, he thought. He nodded. That sounded right. People had camped here since the manager had disappeared. Still, he took the time to find the number of the local police department, call, and suggest that they might want to send someone to check on a group of campers at Shadow Point.

Satisfied that he had done what he could, he pulled back on the road. He passed the diner. He didn't see Martin, but was still sure that the man had noticed his truck going by. He found the Oregon Inn half a mile from the freeway and walked into the lobby. It was bright and cheerful, and made him feel safe the instant he walked inside.

He asked to speak to the manager. A man, looking quite a bit like Martin, emerged from an inner office. "My name is Zach Larson. Your brother Martin recommended this place to me. I'd like to stay here tonight."

"I'm Donovan." The man smiled and took over the registration process himself. "Martin mentioned someone looking like you might be coming over. Shadow Point didn't meet your needs?"

The young woman at the desk looked at Zach like he was crazy. "Shadow Point? Hardly anyone goes there anymore. It's haunted."

"Haunted?" Zach asked. That was one way to look at what he had seen tonight.

"Not by ghosts. Something evil is there." She shuddered. "Good choice on coming here instead."

Donovan handed Zach a key card. "Here you go. I upgraded you to one of our suites. Enjoy."

Zach thanked him and brought in his duffel bag with his clothes and toiletries. He found his room and smiled in relief. At least for tonight, he could pretend to be surrounded by luxury. The bed felt nice, the air conditioner worked, and he could close the heavy curtains and shut out whoever might be watching him.

After showering and changing into pajamas, Zach sat on the couch and looked through the photos he had taken. The hoof prints were nice and clear. In the clearing, he was shocked to see that one of his photos had picked up a tall, shadowy figure standing in front of one of the trees. No face, no clear identifying marks, just a tall, black shadow.

Zach shivered. He was used to looking for cryptids. When he had left home a couple of days ago, he had thought that he was on another Bigfoot hunt with maybe some stories about other creatures thrown in. Now, he had discovered that the legend of a goatman was true and had captured the image of a shadow person. He felt safe for now, but he knew that there could be more danger ahead for him on this trip.

CHAPTER 5

Debbie Thomas watched the truck pulling out of the driveway and noticed the driver staring at them. She saw the sign and shivered. Shadow Point.

Staying here was the idea of both Mark and Steve. The four of them had been working together in Eastern Washington since the end of the college year and needed a break. His aunt, Mariah Dixon, and her wife, Morgan Trent, owned a winery down here in Oregon called Grape Valley. Mark had explained that there was a large festival going on at a bunch of different wineries this weekend. Mariah had arranged for them to stay at a place called Old Forest, in a cabin which had sounded rustic and charming when Debbie looked it up on the website.

Mark had suggested that they camp for a night at Shadow Point on the way down. Steve had promised that they would find a hotel the next night and lounge around, relaxing and swimming, before going down to Old Forest. Tina, the fourth member of their group, had located a tent and some coolers at her family's house. Debbie couldn't see a way to refuse, despite the rumors that this place was haunted.

The first path they drove down led to a site that was already occupied. "Oops," Steve said when two tents appeared in the headlights. At the same time, Debbie saw the hind leg of a deer disappear into the forest.

Mark opened his window. "Hello?"

The tents remained still. One was partially unzipped, but no one looked out at them. Debbie saw no other evidence that people were here. No coolers, no chairs, no logs on the fire pit, and other camping supplies. "This feels weird," she said.

"Yeah," Tina agreed. "Let's go find an empty site."

"Wow, it's dark in here," Steve said as he backed up and crossed the parking lot. They knew that there was currently no manager, and the empty house that they passed looked foreboding. The front door was open, and Debbie noticed what looked like hatchet marks on the wood as the car rolled past the building. Steve pulled into another campsite, stopped the car, and got out to stretch. Mark did the same.

Tina turned to Debbie. "I'm starting to regret this," she whispered.

"I think it's too late. Let's just figure out a way to get through the night and hold them to their promise of a good hotel tomorrow," Debbie responded. She squeezed Tina's hand to reassure the other girl.

Tina nodded. They joined the men outside and quickly got to work to set up their tent. Mark built a fire and Steve turned on a couple of lanterns they had brought with them. They had all just sat down when a rustling in the bushes made them stop speaking.

"What was that?" Tina asked nervously.

"That," a voice replied from the forest. Debbie didn't like that voice. It was low and rough. It sounded like someone who had been drinking and smoking their entire life.

Steve stood. "Come on out here. We're not afraid of you."

"Afraid." A creepy laugh followed that word. Steve marched over to where the voice had come from and started hitting the bushes. Everyone else waited in tense silence.

Nothing happened. Steve shrugged and sat back down. A few minutes later, they heard a car drive through the parking lot. It cruised down the lane that led to their campsite and Debbie was relieved to see the police markings across the vehicle. Two officers stepped out.

"Hey there," one of them said. "How is everything tonight?"

"Good," Mark said.

"It's okay for us to be here, right?" Tina asked. Debbie thought that Tina sounded like she wanted the police to tell them they had to leave.

"It's fine," the other officer said. "We just like to come by now and then to make sure nothing's getting out of hand."

"We're just here for the night," Steve said.

The officer's flashlight landed on Steve's bottle of beer. "Are all of you of legal age?"

They showed him their driver's licenses. "There's another spot across the parking lot with a couple of empty tents. Have you seen anyone else around here?" one of the officers asked.

"Not since we got here," Debbie said. "We thought we heard someone talking just before you arrived though."

"Okay. We'll take another look around and then head out. Have a good night."

"Thanks!" Mark called out as they got into their car and reversed to the parking lot. They turned on their flashing lights so the group could see that they were going around and checking the rest of the campground. When their car was no longer in sight, Debbie squirmed in her seat.

"Tina, want to come with me to the bathroom?" Debbie asked.

"Sure," Tina said reluctantly.

"We'll go when you return," Steve said. "Then it will probably be time for bed."

Tina and Debbie picked up flashlights and walked down the trail to the parking lot. "The tree cover is so heavy," Tina said. "We can't even really see the stars."

Debbie agreed. "It's almost like being someplace other than Earth."

"Don't say that," Tina groaned. They walked into the first door they saw. They were in a cement room, with two stalls, two sinks, and a shower off to the side.

"Check out these locks," Debbie said.

"Out," a low voice responded from the other side of the door. Tina's eyes opened wide. She slammed the bolt and picked up the chain, attaching it to the wall.

"Steve! Mark! Stop playing out there," Debbie shouted.

"Out," the voice repeated.

"I don't think that's the guys," Tina whispered. Debbie looked at her in shock. The two women waited. They heard someone walking around on the gravel, then silence for several minutes.

"You go," Tina said to Debbie in a quiet voice. She did, and then Tina used the bathroom. They washed their hands and released the chain from the wall.

"Ready?" Debbie asked. Tina nodded. They unlocked the door and shined their flashlights outside. Nothing appeared to be waiting for them. They kept their arms linked as they walked back to the campsite.

When they arrived, they found the guys looking quiet and thoughtful. "Why did you throw a hatchet at us?" Mark asked in an intense voice. "What kind of prank is that?"

"Why were you outside the bathroom talking to us?" Tina challenged him.

"What the hell are you talking about?" Steve snapped. "We were sitting right here by the fire when that hatchet flew right past the tent and got stuck in that tree."

They turned to look. Debbie could see a place where a sharp blade had dug into the bark, but there was no hatchet there. "Shit," Mark breathed. He stared at the tree. "It was there just a couple of minutes ago."

"Go," the low voice said, this time loudly and from someplace close to the tent.

Debbie and Tina screamed. Steve sighed, and Mark ran around the tent. "Whoever you are, come out! We're tired of this!"

"Tired," the voice agreed. "Out." Thumping sounds came from the forest. Tina frowned.

"That sounds like hooves," she said quietly. The group waited for the voice to continue, but after a few minutes it appeared their stalker had once again retreated somewhere into the darkness.

"I still have to go to the bathroom," Steve said.

"You're going to leave us here?" Debbie asked anxiously.

"Sit in the car," Mark said. He opened the front door and reached into the glove compartment. He pulled out a pistol. "Let's go, Steve."

"Come on, Debbie," Tina said. The women got into the car and watched anxiously as the men disappeared down the path.

"What is that?" Tina asked after a few minutes of waiting

quietly. She pointed. Debbie saw bushes moving across from them. Shadow Point was living up to its name with the darkness they were facing, and she was not happy with the idea of sharing a campsite with something that spoke from the forest and threw hatchets.

"Let's find out," she said. Mark had left the keys in the ignition. She turned the switch and flicked on the headlights.

The girls screamed, then fell silent in awe of the creature in front of them. It looked like an unnatural combination of man and goat, standing on two legs with large horns coming from its head. It carried a large ax, which it held up so the women could see it clearly. Its red eyes pierced into Debbie's brain.

"Oh my God, we have to get out of here!" she screamed.

Tina opened the door and stepped out of the car. "Where are you going?" Debbie shouted. She saw Tina walk in the direction of the goat monster. Her friend kept her eyes on the creature, seeming to respond to a silent command.

"Hey!" Debbie heard Mark shout. A shot rang out just as Tina reached out her hand to point to the creature. She screamed and the monster disappeared back into the forest.

The men ran over to Tina as Debbie got out of the car. "It was a goat!" she screamed almost incoherently. "It was a goat on two legs, with an ax."

"I don't know what you really saw, but I'm ready to get the hell out of here," Steve said. Mark nodded, guiding Tina back to the car.

They hurried to take down the tent and pack up the car. As they extinguished the lamps, a loud laugh floated through the air. The creature started running in the direction of the campsite. "In the car!" Steve shouted. They dove inside just as the goat monster emerged from the forest, charging at them.

Steve steered as well as he could at a rapid pace on the gravel road. Debbie turned to look at the monster in the glow of the rear lights. She could see its horns and an evil grin on its face as it chased the car. Mark kept his pistol ready, and

Tina curled herself into a ball and buried her face in her hands.

They swung out of Shadow Point and onto the highway. Mark slid the pistol back into the glove compartment, but Steve did not slow down. He had a determined look on his face, and Debbie kept quiet. No one spoke until red and blue lights flashed behind them. Debbie realized numbly that it was already after midnight.

Steve pulled over and waited while an officer came up to his window. "Hello," the same officer they had seen at the campground greeted them. "Decided not to stay the night, I see?"

Mark laughed lightly. "The women wanted something more comfortable than a tent and a sleeping bag."

"Uh huh. Just try to take it a little more slowly, okay? The Oregon Inn is down the road."

"Thanks, officer," Steve said. He got back on the road and took a deep breath. "We don't speak about this to anyone else. Ever."

"They'd think we were crazy," Tina said, finally looking up. "And I almost did go crazy back there. That thing. It was calling to me."

Debbie put an arm around her. "We're all safe now. We'll stay in a hotel for a couple of days, and then we'll be having fun at the winery."

"Fun," Mark replied in a low voice with a grim smile.

"Ha, ha," Debbie said, and rolled her eyes. Steve found the hotel and swung into the parking lot, leaving the car at an odd angle.

"This looks nice," he said quietly. "We can stay here until Thursday and continue with the rest of the trip."

"What if that goat thing followed us?" Tina asked sadly. "It got inside my head. Maybe it knows where we are right now."

"Don't say that," Mark said. "We left it behind at that damn place."

They entered the brightly lit lobby. Debbie and Tina sat in

a couple of soft chairs while Steve and Mark checked into two rooms. When she and Steve reached their room, Debbie sat up after Steve had gone to sleep. She looked in the parking lot and noticed the gray truck she had seen leaving Shadow Point. She wondered what that man had encountered there, and if he was as nervous and scared about it as she was.

CHAPTER 6

When Zach woke up the next morning, he picked up the camera to make sure the images he had captured were still there. Relieved, he showered and went downstairs for breakfast. Donovan was enjoying a cup of coffee and a pastry at a table at the far end of the room. Martin was with him. Zach gathered his breakfast and went over to join them.

"So, you did end up here," Martin said with a smile. "Let me guess. You saw those creepy guys."

"Yes," Zach confirmed. "As well as something I can only describe as part man, part goat."

Martin and Donovan stared at him in silence. "You saw the goatman?" Donovan whispered. "And you survived. Was anyone else there?"

"There were two tents there that I could see, and a car full of people was turning in when I left."

"Some people go out there for a challenge of staying the night," Donovan said. "But you're not the only person Martin has pointed in this direction since the manager went missing."

"I did get some pictures," Zach said. He showed them the images on his camera. Donovan shook his head, and Martin just stared. "Have either of you seen anything like that before?"

"That shadow person. I've seen it," Donovan said. His brother looked at him in surprise. "Down near the wineries a couple of hours away. Especially near Old Forest Cellars. There's something creepy about that area, especially when it gets dark. I was there for a music festival and there were bright lights and people all around me, and yet I always felt like something was out in the vineyard, watching me. When I walked back to my cabin, there was that figure near the edge of the vineyard. It seemed to slink down the edge of the field, almost like a real person, before it disappeared."

"I'm headed to Old Forest Cellars today," Zach said.

"You like this kind of stuff?" Martin asked. Zach nodded

and explained the show to them.

"I've only seen part of one episode," Martin replied. "So, you're hoping to find Bigfoot down in wine country?"

"Not hoping to see it, just looking for evidence," Zach said. He decided not to tell them about his actual experiences with Bigfoot. Among the *Creature Hunt* staff, only Brandon had heard the whole tale and even he had expressed some skepticism that events had actually transpired as Zach had told him.

"Good luck," Donovan said. "That area is going to be packed this weekend."

"It probably was when you were there, too," Zach said. "And yet you saw and felt something."

"What about you, Martin?" Donovan asked. "You see anything strange?"

"Can I see those hoof prints again?" Martin asked. Zach handed him the phone. "Are those new?" he asked.

"Yes. I saw them shortly before I encountered the goatman."

"It's been a year since they found the first prints when the manager disappeared," Martin said. He took another look. "Whatever got him seems to like that spot."

Donovan nodded. "Even before the disappearance, there were stories about weird crap out there. Like that shadow person that's in one of your pictures and the goatman. Those men in suits started showing up after Bill disappeared."

"Have you ever spoken to them?" Zach said. He wished he had brought his notebook down to the breakfast room.

"Yes. The few times that they've shown up in the parking lot here, I went outside and asked if I could help them. They asked some questions about the campground, and said if I saw anything strange to tell them the next time they were in town."

"They come to the diner almost every time they're heading out there," Martin admitted.

"Do they order anything?" Zach asked.

"Yeah, they have lunch or dinner. No alcohol, only water

or soda to drink. I guess that means they're working."

"When do they leave?"

"If it's a quiet night, they tend to stay for about an hour. If there are lots of people in the diner, especially during the summer, they listen for people talking about needing a place to stay for the night. They get up to leave, stop and make a statement about staying away from Shadow Point, and then go out the door. I don't know how many people actually follow their advice, but I'm sure some do. Especially the older crowd."

Zach nodded. Donovan looked at his watch. "I better get to the desk. Zach, I extended your check-out time to as late as one o'clock if you need it. Just come by the desk on your way out to drop off your key."

"Thank you. For the food and the information." Zach put his trash in a container on his way out the door and took the stairs up to the second floor. Once he was back in the room, he sat and wrote down as much of the conversation as he could remember. He saved the camera photos to his computer as well as a flash drive, then placed the flash drive in his duffel bag. He had learned to back up evidence as often as possible.

His cell phone rang as he was reading through the Bigfoot Online Group forum, a website dedicated to Bigfoot sightings and stories. Autumn was a member. She had not posted much lately, but he had a feeling that she had probably caught up on the forum at some point during her travels on Monday.

"Hey, sweetie," he answered when he saw it was Autumn. "How's the library conference?"

"Small, so far. The main stuff picks up tomorrow into the weekend. How's Oregon?"

"You won't believe what happened last night." He filled her in on Shadow Point, stopping at the diner, going to the campsite, and what he had found. "The goatman was huge, larger than I expected it to be. It had reddish eyes. When it looked at me, I felt there was only evil inside its head. It had large horns, carried a weapon, and didn't want me there."

"So, you ran out of the house and stayed to look around the rest of the site. And you didn't look in the tents?"

Zach paused. "No. I just assumed someone was inside, and I didn't want to disturb them."

"Some people on BOG claim that sightings of Bigfoot are sometimes accompanied by shadow figures or men dressed all in black."

"I know." Zach had encountered that once before while filming the show, which was why he didn't think these two men following him were any type of paranormal entity.

It had happened after their search for the Jersey Devil had left Brandon with some unexplained scratches on his back. While the cameraman was being examined by a paramedic, Zach had noticed a man in a black suit appear out of nowhere, look around, glance over the paramedic's shoulder, and then disappear. He had not said a word, but Zach had seen him get into a car with another person, a woman, waiting in the passenger seat. He had never told Brandon about it.

"Anyway, I'm checking out of here soon and heading down to Old Forest Cellars. I'll be staying there for a few days. Cell service may be spotty so don't panic if you can't reach me."

"No problem. Oh, I have to go. Lunch meeting with a few people. Love you."

"Love you, too." Zach hung up and returned to the Bigfoot message board. He searched for goatmen and was surprised to see a subforum about that. Most people who thought they had seen one agreed that it had terrified them. There were links that led him to other goatman sightings, and he got caught up in research.

A glance at his watch showed him it was time to get back on the road. He turned off the computer and packed. When he left the room, he glanced around one more time to make sure he had everything. Assured that he did, he walked down to the front desk. Donovan came over and accepted his key.

"Don't let my experience keep you from enjoying Old Forest and the other wineries," he said. "They're all good people down there and it's going to be busy."

"Good," Zach said. "Maybe that means people won't notice what I'm doing."

He said goodbye to Donovan and packed up his truck. For a moment, he considered driving back to Shadow Point. He looked around the lot and saw that the car with the four young adults from last night was parked awkwardly near the entrance, almost taking up two complete spots. He could imagine the driver speeding in here, looking for a safe shelter after experiencing something at the campground.

He backed up. As he was ready to leave the parking lot, he looked out the window and saw one of the black-suited men standing under the hotel sign. He shook his head at Zach, and Zach simply waved. He wasn't going to let anyone keep him from finding cryptids. He drove away. When he looked back in his mirror, the space under the sign was empty.

CHAPTER 7

After driving through the town of Vineville and stopping to replenish his cooler, Zach reached Old Forest Cellars mid-afternoon and pulled into the main parking lot. Three buildings surrounded the pavement. One was a large two-story house that appeared to have been converted into offices. There was also a one-story brick building fronted by a large patio where people were sitting at tables enjoying glasses of wine. A sign near the door proclaimed this to be the tasting rom. The third structure was a large pavilion with a cement floor, raised stage, and several picnic tables. Zach guessed that this was where the bands would be playing for the music portions of the festival this weekend.

Between the pavilion and the house was a large, round pond with lots of weeds around it. A fence had been constructed to keep people away from the edges, but at one side an opening in the fence led to a long dock that reached out almost halfway across the pond. He saw a few people sitting on the dock, their legs in the water, chatting and drinking.

Beyond the buildings, he could see vast fields of grapes tucked onto wood trellises. A path that started just outside the tasting room had a sign with "Cabins this way" printed on it. Zach could see the forest behind the vineyards. It appeared to be almost as dark and foreboding as Shadow Point. He hoped that the goatman would not find its way down here.

He got out of the truck and headed for the tasting room. Three people wearing shirts with the Old Forest logo were busy serving and discussing wines with the customers. Zach entered the room and found it pleasantly cool. It was larger than he had expected. Stools lined a counter, and several tables were scattered around inside. T-shirts and other Old Forest Cellars souvenirs were on display against one of the walls. Another wall had a menu of all the wines currently being tasted and available to buy. "Hi, welcome to Old Forest Cellars," said a dark-skinned man behind the counter.

"My name is Damon. How can I help you?"

"I'm here to see Nancy Dakota," Zach said.

The man turned around to an open doorway behind him. "Nancy! Someone is asking for you!"

A woman appeared in the doorway, wearing jeans and another shirt with the Old Forest logo. She was average height, somewhere in her forties, with short brown hair and eyes. She was tan and sturdily built, looking as if she spent a lot of time out in the vineyards. "Hi. Zach Larson?"

"That's me." She came around the counter and shook his hand. He saw Damon's eyes widen at the mention of Zach's name and wondered if Tasha had said anything to her co-workers about his arrival.

"Let me show you to your cabin." Four more people entered the room, and Damon turned his attention to them. Zach followed Nancy out the front door, through the busy patio, and onto the dirt path that wound around the back of the building and past one of the fenced vineyards. The path led down a small hill that offered the cabins some privacy from the people wandering around the rest of the property.

"Tasha mentioned you were down here doing research for a book," Nancy said.

"Yes. I've heard some interesting stories already on this trip. And when I looked up this winery on some travel websites, a few people mentioned that they've heard there's a creature around here that could be Bigfoot, or a dogman."

Nancy laughed. "That's what Tasha seems to think. Damon, too. You might want to talk to him later."

"I'd love to be able to talk to anyone who might have seen something."

Nancy stopped walking. "There's going to be a lot of people down here starting tomorrow. As you saw, I do a lot of business even without the twice-yearly festivals we have. I don't want to scare any of those people away from here."

"That's not my intention. I'm here to document any evidence I can find and interview people who are willing to talk to me." He smiled at her. "I don't think any monster I'm looking for would appear when there are a lot of people gathered. From my experiences, most cryptids would rather be left alone."

"Let's hope so." Nancy resumed walking. They reached a clearing with seven cabins. She led him to the last one. It was about thirty feet from the others and the only thing next to it, on the other side of a gravel road, was another field of grape vines. Zach could already sense that anything could be hiding in that field, watching them.

"Here's your cabin." She pulled a key from her pocket and opened the door. Zach stepped inside and was happy to see that it was slightly more well-furnished than Tasha had described. The bed was already made with sheets and a comforter, and a blanket was neatly folded on the end. An air conditioning unit was attached to the wall, and one window looked out over the field while the other one had a view of the other cabins. The bathroom was small, but included a shower.

"There are towels and extra linens in the closet," Nancy said. She told Zach the price per night, and he nodded. It was very reasonable. "There's only the fridge and the microwave, but I imagine you'll probably be out most of the time."

Zach nodded. There was a table and two chairs with a lamp as well as a nightstand with another lamp. A television sat on a table in the corner across from the bed.

"Does the internet work down here?"

"Absolutely. The password is on that card on the table."

Zach took another look around. "This is perfect. Thank you for saving it for me."

"We don't usually have meals, but this weekend we have both breakfast and dinner service here. They're simple buffets, but are included in the price of the cabin, and in the price of the festival for people staying just for the day or setting up tents down by the office and pavilion. That starts in the morning, though, so you're on your own for dinner tonight." She pointed to a binder on the nightstand. "Lots of dining options in Vineville and Albany are included."

"Thanks. I drove through downtown Vineville on my way out here and saw some restaurants. Can I park my truck down here?"

"Sure. When you leave the parking lot, turn left. You'll see this gravel road about a quarter of a mile down marked for Old Forest guests only. Turn left onto it, and that'll bring you right here." They stepped outside, and Zach noticed a strip of gravel by each cabin. "Only one vehicle allowed per unit."

"No problem. I'll go ahead and get settled in. Would there be a good time to interview some of your staff members?"

Nancy checked her watch. "We close the tasting room today at five, in an hour. Damon will be free then, and he's probably the person with the most information other than Elizabeth, the office manager. Elizabeth lives over the office, on the second floor. I have the third floor."

"That must be convenient."

"It is. And it's more private than you might think. When people arrive here, they're directed right to the tasting room, and the office is really for the behind-the-scenes work of the winery. It's a very nice location, and the wineries down here tend to work together to get customers to each other. We all have different wines and benefit from people touring the valley."

"I'll be sure to visit a couple of the others while I'm here."

Nancy smiled. "You won't regret it. I have to get back to the tasting room. I'm sure I'll see you around later." She left the key on the table and closed the door behind her.

Zach took in his surroundings. He could not have asked for a better situation for staying up late to see if any monsters showed themselves. The other six cabins were far enough away that he had some privacy, but close enough that he could run for help if he was so inclined. He took another look out at the vineyard and the memory of his goatman encounter ran through his head.

After getting settled in and cleaning out some trash from his truck, Zach placed his notebook, his camera, and his cell phone in his backpack. After looking out at the vineyard, he also included the knife and a can of bear spray. He walked over to the tasting room and found Nancy and Damon finishing their cleaning.

"Do you have time to answer a few questions?" Zach asked Damon.

"Sure." He looked over at Nancy. She smiled and nodded. "Let's go sit outside."

"Would you like a glass of wine?" Nancy asked. "Free for you today. You'll have to pay the rest of the time."

Zach smiled. "Sure. Chardonnay, please."

"I'll bring it out."

Zach followed Damon to a table underneath a dark green canopy. Everyone who had been here earlier had left, and the silence was peaceful. Damon settled into his chair with a bottle of water.

"Tasha mentioned you. She was impressed that her husband is working on the show you host, and she said you were really into Bigfoot and stuff like that."

"I am." Zach took out his notebook and phone. "Can I record this?"

"Sure."

Zach wrote down Damon's name, the place, and the time, then spoke it all out loud for the recorder. "How long have you been working here?"

"Three years." He took a deep breath. "I made some mistakes when I was eighteen and served two years in jail. Nancy agreed to take on me and a couple of other former inmates when we were released as part of a work program. The others left soon after, and I lost touch with them. I worked up from janitor, to learning the accounting software, to running the tasting room." He took a sip of water. "I'm telling you all this so you know that Nancy trusts me. I'm hoping you will, as well."

"Thank you for your honesty," Zach said. Nancy appeared with two glasses of wine and a plate of cheese and crackers. She handed Zach his glass, then quietly sat down at the table with them to listen to the interview.

"Have you ever experienced anything that you think would be paranormal, or unexplained? Have you ever seen anything that you would consider to be an unusual creature for this area?"

Damon nodded. "In the first few months that I worked here, I slept in one of the cabins out back. After the other two men left, I was out there alone. One December evening, I walked back there after cleaning up from a wine tasting. It was about this time of day and already dark. I noticed that a large dog seemed to gotten onto the property and was walking along the fence line. It had kind of a strange gait and its eyes were brighter than any dog I'd ever seen."

"Can you tell me more about the dog?"

"It was brown, with some gray hair along the back. I saw later that there was also some gray along the belly. I stood there, kind of transfixed by the sight of it, and found myself moving over to the field where the dog had stopped. It went into the vines, and I almost followed. It was like something was pulling me."

Zach tried to keep his emotions out of his voice. "What happened then?"

"I turned my head and looked down the road that leads to the forest. There were shadowy figures standing there. No human or animal features, just shadows. At first, I thought they were my former co-workers coming back to play a prank, but they just stared at me in silence. I couldn't see any eyes, but it still felt like they were looking into my head. Finally, I heard a voice come from one of them and I was close enough to hear his tone. It was dark and menacing. He told me that I would soon be seeing evil."

"Seeing evil," Zach repeated. Nancy shook her head, a worried look in her eyes. A glance off to the right made her pause. Two cars had pulled into the parking lot and one of the passengers was waving at her. She waved back and Zach saw a slim woman in an Old Forest shirt approach the car.

"Let me just interrupt this for a minute," Nancy said. "Old

Forest is a strange place. Many Native American tribes in the area have described it as an evil place, and they won't go in there. The owners of Grape Valley, Legends, and myself have put warnings up on the tall fence that runs along the back of our properties. Gates are kept locked, and few people have the keys."

"We check on the gates from time to time," Damon added. "Elizabeth volunteers to do that quite often. I think she likes to hang out near there, hoping to see something."

"I've heard strange calls and what sounds like wood knocking on trees," Nancy said. Zach's eyes widened as he took notes. "There's a mist that often appears in there, and places that are cold even on the hottest summer days. I'm telling you this so you realize why we try to stay out of there."

"Thank you," Zach replied.

She pointed at the people who were now standing by the pavilion. "I have a meeting with some people about this weekend. I'll take them into the office." She walked away, and Zach turned back to Damon.

"What happened after you saw the shadow people?" he asked.

"I looked back at the vineyard, and the dog emerged from the vines. This time, it was walking on its hind legs and I finally noticed how large its paws were. They looked like they could easily rip my head from my body." Damon shook his head. "You hear a lot about Bigfoot down here. I know what that supposedly looks like. This was not Bigfoot."

"What did it look like at that point?"

"Its face was still very much like a dog, with a long snout, but it had a broad chest. Its eyes glowed without any other light around to cause a reflection. Two ears were sticking up on the top of its head. I first I thought they were horns, but then one of them twitched like the creature had heard something." Damon closed his eyes and squeezed the table. "I hate to say the word, but it was a dogman."

"What happened next?"

"I backed away from it and looked down the road. Those shadowy figures were gone, and when I dared to turn to the field again, the monster was gone too." Damon swallowed. "That was the first time."

"How many times have you seen it since then?"

"Five. The last time I saw it was in March. Tasha heard it, out behind the tasting room. She didn't know what it was, but she knew that something tall was lurking out in the vineyard and she could see the outline of the head. She ran back inside and insisted I walk her out to her car." Damon smiled. "I knew what it was, didn't want to scare her. I told her it was probably just a few local guys trespassing and assured her I'd report it to Nancy."

"And did you?"

"Of course. I tell her every time I see it." He looked down at the plate and took a cracker, then bit into it and chewed slowly. Zach waited patiently, taking a few bites of cheese himself. "I would think that we'll have at least one report this weekend of someone seeing it. Maybe it's just that there are more people here for the festivals and that increases the chances of sightings. Or maybe this creature wants to hunt humans and knows it has a better selection around this time of year."

"What about in December? Is there anything big going on down here?"

"Holiday lights," Damon replied. "All the wineries do big displays and offer food and case discounts. Even if it's been snowing, people like to come down and get ready for the holidays."

"So, again, more people than usual."

"I wonder if this thing is actually really an animal. Maybe it just comes from some other dimension, or from hell," Damon said. "If it's always here, why doesn't it appear to us more?"

"Could be that it moves around the area to look for food," Zach suggested. If there was a dogman here, it would need a space to hide in somewhere in the forests around the winery.

"Have you ever seen those shadow people again?"

"Once or twice. And a couple of times, these weird dudes in black suits and sunglasses have shown up here. They stand at the edge of the patio and ignore everyone. When I appear at the door, they turn and walk away."

"Interesting," Zach noted. "You've given me a lot to think about. One more question."

"What's that?"

"Have you ever seen Bigfoot?"

Damon laughed, but in a way that invited Zach to laugh with him. "A dogman's not strange enough for you? Naw, I haven't seen Bigfoot. Maybe even he's scared of whatever this is, although you do hear stories now and then of people who claim they've seen large footprints around here."

"What about paw prints?"

"Only once, and that was Elizabeth who saw them. She runs the office and does the bookkeeping."

"I'm sure I'll be talking to her soon." Zach turned off the recorder and drank more of his wine. He and Damon sat and chatted about the winery for a few minutes. Once Zach was done with his glass, they both stood to signal an end to the conversation.

"Do you know where I can get dinner around here? Nancy left some suggestions in the cabin, but do you recommend any place in particular?"

"There's a tavern down the road at Grape Valley. They're open until ten."

"Thank you, Damon."

"You're welcome. See you tomorrow, Zach."

Zach walked back to his cabin and placed his bag on the table. He then took a shower, went to his truck to locate Grape Valley on his GPS, and set out for dinner. On his way down the road, he saw something large, with brown fur, disappear into the forest across from the winery. He shook his head and kept going.

CHAPTER 8

When Zach reached Grape Valley, he found the tavern easily. The scent of good food floated out to the parking lot, which seemed almost empty for nearly seven o'clock on a summer evening. He stepped inside and looked around, noting that the dining area seemed to be only half-full.

"Hi there! Please choose a table and someone will be right with you," a waitress called out as she walked by with a full tray. Zach chose a table that looked out on the parking lot, where he could clearly see his truck. It was still light outside, and he was glad he had come down here in the warm days of June rather than the cold, darker days of December.

"Here's a menu," the same waitress said, interrupting his thoughts. She also placed a glass of water on the table. "We're starting our evening wine specials tonight. Three dollars per glass after seven."

He smiled. The wine at Old Forest had been nice. He should try something here. He ordered a glass of red wine and checked out the menu while also looking around at the other restaurant guests. They all seemed to be immersed in their food and private conversations.

When his wine arrived, he placed his order and then leaned back, sipped, and relaxed. The tavern was decorated with solid dark wood walls, oak tables and chairs, and a beautifully shined bar. There was a gas fireplace near him, but when he got up and put his hand near the glass door, he discovered that no heat was coming from it. Still, it contributed to the cozy atmosphere of the dining room.

He looked around and realized that the wall had a rack of brochures about wineries in the area. He grabbed a few and sat back down. Grape Valley was on the top of pile, so he read about the vineyard started twenty years ago by Mariah Dixon and Morgan Trent, two women who appeared to be a couple from the way they were holding hands in one of the photos. He recognized them as two of the people waiting for Nancy back at Old Forest. The brochure for Old

Forest Cellars was next on the stack, and he smiled at the pictures of people having fun in the pavilion and relaxing on the patio. No mention was made of the forest, and he realized that the staff probably tried to be careful about promoting it to tourists.

When his food arrived, he set the brochures aside and ate. After he finished his wine, he declined a second glass and instead drank another glass of water. When he had paid and left a generous tip, he took the pile of paper with him and went back out to his truck.

He was just opening the door when he sensed he was being watched. He grabbed a flashlight from the glove box and locked the truck. Just beyond the tavern was a small creek, and he saw a fence running along the opposite bank. Some bushes shook, and then the animals he had been hearing went silent.

Three cars pulled into the parking lot. Zach waited as the arriving guests entered the tavern, then rushed over to the creek. He remembered it from the map. It also ran through Legends, the other vineyard bordering Old Forest. The chain link fence had been overtaken by foliage in some places, but it was still visible. He could also see the discreet signs warning people to stay away. The signs were made of wood and styled to look as natural as possible.

He pointed the flashlight across the creek. Nothing reflected back, no animal appeared, and as he stood still, he heard crickets start chirping again. He waited. "Hello?" he called out, trying not to draw the attention of other people. Frustrated, he picked up a log from a pile of firewood and hit a nearby tree three times. He waited for a response.

None came, but he once again felt like he was being watched. He dropped the log and turned. A tall, dark shape stood at the edge of the creek, just a few feet away.

Zach gasped. Even this close, he couldn't make out much about the shadow person. It stood still, with a shape that suggested a suit and a hat on its head. It turned, and its solid face seemed to study him. Zach closed his eyes, and when he opened them the shadow person was gone.

"Time to leave," he muttered, and ran back to his truck. Most people would probably blame this sighting on alcohol, but he had been very careful so far about his wine consumption. He'd definitely be having a couple of beers in his cabin later.

When he reached Old Forest Cellars, he drove past the main lot and parked beside his cabin. There were lights on and voices in the distance. It sounded like Nancy and her guests were at the patio. Remembering Nancy's welcome earlier, he decided to take a chance on going up there and maybe finding another staff member to talk to about sightings.

When he reached the patio, he found Nancy there with about seven other people. "Hi, Zach!" she called out. "I spoke with Elizabeth. She'll be in the office until ten if you'd like to ask her some questions."

"I would," Zach said. "Thank you."

"You're Zach Larson!" one of the men said, and stood. A woman sitting next to him reached out and held on to his shirt, and Zach could see he might have had a bit too much alcohol. He reached out and shook Zach's hand. "I'm a big fan of the show."

"Thank you."

"On a vacation?" asked one of the women that Zach had seen before he left for dinner. He realized that she was Morgan Trent, one of the owners of Grape Valley. Mariah Dixon was seated next to her, leaning back in her chair with her arms crossed, looking as if she had been in the middle of an argument.

"Something like that. A working vacation. My girlfriend and I are writing a book about investigating cryptids."

"Not much down here," said another man. He shook his head. "Never seen anything strange."

"Give it some time. You've only been at your place for a year," Nancy said. She smiled at Zach. "See you tomorrow."

It was a polite dismissal, so Zach took the hint and left.

He walked over to the house that included the winery office. As he passed the pavilion, dark and empty tonight, a motion sensor light startled him. He wondered how many more of those were located on the grounds.

He opened the building door and found himself in a long hallway. At the end of the hall a doorway marked "Private" probably led to the second and third floors. Four other doors were located along the corridor. One of them, just off to his right, was open. "Hello?" he called out.

A woman appeared in the doorway, and he realized she was the staff member who had greeted the guests in the parking lot. Tall and blonde, she had clear blue eyes that sparkled when she saw him and smiled. "Hi," she said. "I'm Elizabeth Monroe. Nancy mentioned you might be over tonight."

"Zach Larson," he said. She shook his hand.

"Come in to my office," she said. "Are you down here alone?"

"Yes. My girlfriend wasn't able to make it on this trip."

He thought her smile faded slightly when he mentioned Autumn, but she covered it well. "We're glad you here. Damon mentioned that he told you about seeing a dogman."

"Do you believe him?" Zach asked. He sat down across from her as she returned to a chair behind her desk.

"Yes." She gestured to the bookcase behind him. He turned and saw two full rows of books relating to cryptozoology. He recognized the names of several of the authors, some of whom he had interviewed for the show. "Cryptozoology is an interest of mine. I minored in Biology for fun at college."

"What was your major?"

"Business." She gestured out the window. "I guess I just happened to land in an area where I could indulge in both work and hobby at the same time."

"Have you seen the dogman?"

"No. I even tried to stake out one of the fields last December. Not the one where Damon saw him, but the field closest to the pavilion here. Nothing happened on either night that I was out there."

"Have you seen anything else around here?"

"Not personally. Some people say they've seen Bigfoot. I ask them if they've been over to Legends Vineyard and they almost always admit they have. Then, driving back here in the dark and seeing the woods, their mind is already on large hairy monsters."

"What's over at Legends?"

"You should go there tomorrow and see for yourself." She smiled. "I don't want to influence you before you have a chance to explore."

"Nancy said you'll be busy here this weekend."

"Yep, but that doesn't stop strange things from happening, or strange creatures from making an appearance." She shrugged.

"Do you have any unexplained disappearances around here?"

"Funny you should ask." She got up and retrieved a binder from the bookcase. Her eagerness to be helpful reminded him a lot of Autumn, and he suddenly missed her deeply.

"I've been keeping track of sightings in the ten years I've been working here. This binder has a collection of sightings by staff and guests. It seems like after every big festival, there are reports of between five and ten people that end up being reported as missing to the police over in Albany, so I've also added a section about people who have mysteriously disappeared. I've been able to locate some of them because they visited here and I can call them on a pretense of winery business, either offering a discount online or a reduced rate for the next event. Anna Ryan over at Legends has been able to find a few people, as well. But there are always some that neither of us can find."

"Maybe they just eventually showed up at home and never came back here again. Would the police tell you if they heard from them?"

Elizabeth brought the binder to her desk. "I think so. We

do have a connection to the police. Damon's uncle Marcus is a detective in Albany, and he's usually the one to follow up on the missing person cases. He used to be a skeptic about Damon's monster stories, but he wouldn't cover something up if he thought it would be helpful."

"Do you know him personally?"

Elizabeth nodded. "He'll be here tomorrow, actually. He helps oversee the security guards that Nancy hires for the weekend."

"You say he used to be a skeptic?"

"I think he had an experience that changed his mind. He doesn't say much about it, but the last time I saw him he didn't laugh at my book collection like he usually does."

Zach nodded and gestured to the binder. "Can I look at that?"

Elizabeth handed it to him and silently returned to her work. As she started typing something on her computer, Zach browsed through the notebook. Just as she had said, she had included written statements from Damon about what he had seen, her own experiences and statements from other employees, and information about the missing people. "How many of these people were actually staying here when they were reported missing?"

"Six," she replied promptly without looking away from her screen. "There's no pattern to it. One year we had one missing guest, last year there were three."

"Damon mentioned two former convicts who had left after being here for a couple of months."

She looked over at him and frowned. "I haven't thought about them in awhile."

"You don't know where they ended up?"

"Nancy warned the other winery owners around here about them. Not in a criminal sense, just that they hadn't been reliable workers for her. As far as I know, they didn't try to find jobs locally."

"Be nice to know if they ended up somewhere," Zach said. "As opposed to maybe being victims of the dogman."

Elizabeth gave him her full attention again. "Do you think it got a taste of blood and realized this could be a feeding ground?"

"From my experience with seeing them in action, it's a flesh and blood monster. It would need sustenance at some point. That's the theory most Bigfoot hunters use when they're looking for large hairy apes. They'll set food out as part of a trap."

She pulled up a calendar online. "Let's see. Damon started here a little over three and a half years ago, in October. The other two guys left in December."

"Is that when a lot of dogman sightings started?"

"It wasn't for another year that reports of sightings become more frequent." Elizabeth looked down at her desk. "I wonder if it's always been in this area, but just needed some sort of motivation to come into the winery and look for people."

"Nancy mentioned there's a fence keeping people out of the forest."

"Yeah, but that doesn't mean whatever's in the forest can't get through or over that fence."

"Have there been any reported physical attacks?"

"Oh my God," Elizabeth said softly. "I didn't think about that. Yes, but it's always been assumed that people fell, or got scratched by a fence, or some other more plausible explanation. I never believed that a dogman would kill a human here."

"It's okay," he assured her. "I doubt anyone would believe that. Most of the time, people just report sightings. And it's likely that if a dogman does kill someone, it's away from other human eyes."

She looked down at her desk again. She played with the handle of one of the drawers, biting her lower lip. She looked up and smiled, then rubbed her eyes. "Sorry, Zach. This is really interesting, but I'm tired and tomorrow is the start of our festival. Artists, merchants, and musical acts are going to be filling our time for the next three days."

"That's okay. Would you mind making a copy of this book for me tonight or tomorrow? I'd like to look through these pages again. I have my own notes from Damon but a second account is always good."

"Sure," she agreed. He stood and shook her hand. "I look forward to helping you with whatever I can while you're here, Zach."

"Me, too."

He left the office and walked back across the parking lot. The light came on again, and this time he stopped. He could swear that something tall and dark had jumped out of the way, just beyond his field of vision. He waited a full minute until the light went off, then stood still.

It was there. Nothing that he could define, just a dark shape. He considered a shadow person, but wondered if they would have the capability of triggering a motion sensor. He turned, and the light went on again. He continued on his way. When he passed the tasting room, he saw that Nancy's meeting had broken up. He heard voices inside the building and assumed that she was inside taking care of some last-minute details for the morning.

He found the path to the cabins. When he entered his room, he closed the door and immediately opened his laptop. He was very interested in Elizabeth's stories and wanted to document their conversation. After he was satisfied with his work, he stretched and checked his phone for messages.

A loud voice made him look out the window at the other cabins. They were empty tonight, except for the one closest to him. A truck had pulled up nearly sideways next to it, and he recognized the man who had spoken to him earlier. He opened the door and stepped out onto the porch. "Hey!" the man shouted with a wave and a slurred voice. "Looks like we're neighbors tonight."

"Bob, quiet down," the woman with him scolded as she appeared in the doorway to help the man inside. "We decided to stay for the night," she explained to Zach in a softer voice.

"Probably a good idea," he said.

"Pretty dark out here!" the man exclaimed. There were lights along the path, but they were nowhere near as bright as the ones up closer to the tasting room and office. "Bet we see Bigfoot tonight!"

"Oh, yeah?" Zach asked politely. He was getting tired and seeing his cabin door behind him was making him anxious to get inside and get to sleep.

"Yep. Make sure you put that in your show." The man winked at him and went inside. His wife smiled, wished Zach a good night, and closed the door.

Zach smiled. Despite the fact that there was possibly an evil monster attacking people here, the people he had met so far had been incredibly helpful. That wasn't always the case when he had traveled to other small towns for the show.

He took a shower and changed into pajamas. It was too late to call Autumn, but he sent her a few texts and a couple of pictures. He'd get a response in the morning, probably with some stories and pictures of her own. He smiled and got into bed.

After he turned off the light, he was immediately aware of a brightness beyond the door. He got out of bed and looked at the other cabins. A motion sensor light was in the tree next to the cabin across from where the other couple was staying. He waited until it went off again, but didn't see anything. He shook his head and returned to bed.

After Zach left her office, Elizabeth stretched and thought about the television personality. She had formed a crush on him from the first episode of the show, and was disappointed to hear he was dating someone. At least, she thought, she could try to spend some time with him while he was down here.

She opened the bottom drawer of her desk. A skeletal paw rested on a towel inside a cardboard box. She touched the paw, then folded the towel back over it and carefully shut the drawer.

She had found the paw two years ago. On one of her trips

beyond the fence, she had followed a trail that disappeared into a light mist. It had led to a shelter made of fallen trees. She had also noticed a circle of stones. The paw, large and with unusual digits extending from the center, had been just inside the circle.

Elizabeth had taken it and ran. She had heard something following her on the path, but was able to get to the fence and lock it. By the time she gathered up the courage to turn and face the forest, she had barely seen a brownish-haired animal retreating in the forest on four legs.

The paw had been moved a couple of times. She kept it here with the rest of her collection. She looked at the drawer again and wondered if she should try to return the paw to the forest. Maybe the creature who had died had relatives that were now looking for its remains.

She made a copy of every page in the notebook and put the pages together in a different binder. She placed a note with Zach's name on it and stuck it on the table near her door. She was tired, but not yet ready for bed. Instead, she walked out the front door and over to the patio, where Nancy's meeting with the owners of Legends, Grape Valley, and a couple of other wineries had already ended.

"Hi, Anna. Hi, Bob," she greeted the owners of Legends Vineyard, about ten miles down the road from Old Forest. They were just coming out of the tasting room and Bob appeared to be weaving as he walked across the patio.

"Another night of enjoying our products a bit too much?" Elizabeth asked Anna quietly. Nancy emerged from the building and approached Bob, speaking to him in a soft voice.

"He saw it again last night," Anna said. Elizabeth gasped. The dogman that seemed to have found a home at Old Forest had also discovered Legends. "He still claims that it's just a small Bigfoot. I don't think he can really imagine a wolf walking upright."

"But you have a statue of a werewolf," Elizabeth pointed out. "And an entire dining area centered around it." Creatures like Bigfoot were the entire theme of Legends. She knew for a fact that Bob sometimes played pranks with guests using a special footprint cast he owned, and often told bold, and made up, stories about his own encounters.

"Yeah, designed from a monster movie. There's something real out there." Anna was very matter-of-fact about monsters. She believed they existed, but preferred to not have them close to her.

Nancy guided Bob back over to them. "You said you were exhausted, and Bob shouldn't drive. Why don't you two stay here tonight?"

"Are you sure?" Anna asked. "It's not too far to drive, but I admit it would be nice to be in a bed in a few minutes."

"Yep. Elizabeth, would you get the key for Cabin 6?"

"Sure." Elizabeth turned and hurried back to the office. She entered the building and found the key hanging behind Nancy's desk. On her way back, she saw something out of the corner of her eye that stopped her mid-stride.

A wolf with glowing yellow eyes sat at the edge of the vineyard. It held a dead animal in its two front paws, which were massive and ended in long fingers. It took a bite from the creature, then looked up and saw Elizabeth. She heard a growl and gasped.

The dogman stood up on its hind legs, and Elizabeth realized how well the creature could hide in the vast fields of grapes. It was just slightly taller than the vines, roughly six feet, and down on all fours it could slink around quietly and attack before anyone knew they were being followed. On its hind legs, it looked like a dog standing up for a trick. This creature, though, had good balance and seemed comfortable on two legs. It turned and walked away into the field, carrying its dinner with it.

Elizabeth heard Nancy calling her and continued on to the patio. "Sorry," she said. She tried to hide the mix of fear and excitement in her voice. "Cabin 6, Anna. You're next to our new guest, Zach Larson."

"Great!" Bob exclaimed.

"Let's get the truck and drive down there," Anna said. "We'll be out early, Nancy."

"Just leave the key in the mail box," Nancy said. "Good night."

The Ryans left. Nancy shut off the lights and Elizabeth joined her to walk back to their home. Along the way, she looked over at the vineyard. She saw nothing. "Everything okay?" Nancy asked.

"Yep. Just thinking about this weekend."

"Marcus will be here around noon to get the security guys organized. Other than that, I think we're ready."

"Yes," Elizabeth agreed. They chatted for a few minutes in the downstairs hall of the building, then Nancy went up to her apartment. Elizabeth took a few minutes to sit down in her office and write out her sighting, made a copy for both notebooks, and then headed up to her own apartment. She was relieved to finally close and lock the door behind her.

She took a quick shower, then turned off her bedroom light. She sat on the window seat and glanced out over the winery. From this vantage point, she could barely see the cabins out behind the tasting room. All the property lights were off, except for a few lights along the path between the office and the parking lot. The silence was almost unnerving. She slipped into bed and thought about Zach until she fell asleep.

CHAPTER 9

When Zach woke up early the next morning, he felt uneasy. There was nothing about the inside of the cabin that was out of place. He shuffled to the door and listened for movement, but couldn't hear anything. He opened the door and grabbed a piece of paper that had just been taped to the frame by an Old Forest employee, who was already retreating out of the cabin area.

The paper was a schedule of the weekend's events, along with a daily weather forecast. A buffet breakfast was listed as being open in the tasting room in an hour or so. He thought it would be lightly attended, since as far as he knew only one other cabin had been occupied last night.

To be sure, he glanced outside. The other truck was still parked outside the nearest cabin. A light mist was already being chased away by the sun. He looked at the schedule and saw that the forecast for today was clear and in the mid-eighties.

He showered and dressed, then made himself a cup of coffee. He sat at the table and thought about his conversation with Elizabeth last night. She certainly seemed to know a lot about cryptids, and he hoped that the information she had shown him last night would be useful. He was already thinking about how to include this investigation in the book. Autumn, although interested in other creatures, had always been strongly focused on Bigfoot. Zach figured it was up to him to add some variety to the chapters, and this would be an interesting diversion.

He heard voices outside and opened the door. The drunk man from the previous night had opened his vehicle and appeared to be looking for something. Zach ventured out to the front porch. "Hi!" he called.

The man turned around, saw Zach, and pushed at something inside the truck. He closed the door and waved at Zach. His hands were empty. "Hey there, neighbor. Did you see it too?"

"See what?" Zach asked.

The man pointed to the ground between the two cabins. "Bigfoot."

Zach was ready to roll his eyes. He looked at where the man had pointed and sighed in disbelief. There were several large footprints in the dirt. They started at the edge of the grass between the two cabins and stopped at the gravel road.

"Did you see what made those?" he asked. He held up a hand to stop the man before he could respond. He stepped back inside the cabin, grabbed his camera, and carefully walked over to where the tracks began. The man, joined now by his wife, stayed out of the way.

"It was large and hairy," the woman said. She had closed the door behind them. She opened the truck long enough to place an overnight bag inside, and Zach saw a large wooden board underneath the rear window. A long object was mounted to it. He couldn't see enough to identify the object, though.

"What time was this?" Zach asked as he followed the tracks, taking pictures all the way. He stopped at the road and wondered why the tracks didn't appear in the patches of dirt on the other side. Right across from his cabin was an empty area that had probably once held another building, and beyond that was the fenced vineyard.

"A little after one," the woman said. "It was walking slowly and looked at us when we were watching it through our window."

Zach nodded. "This is interesting."

"Not the first time I've seen a Bigfoot," the man said. He didn't seem inclined to introduce himself, although he had made sure that Zach knew he was aware of the television show last night.

"Honey, we should be going."

"Oh, right." The man waved. "Maybe we'll see you later."

Zach smiled and waved back. He returned to his cabin and saved the pictures to his laptop and hard drive. He then sent them to Autumn. To his surprise, she called him right away.

"Where are those?" she asked after greeting him.

"Right outside the cabin. The fellow who stayed there last night was nice enough to point them out to me and even claimed he saw the creature that made them."

"Do you believe him?"

"He was pretty drunk when I saw him late last night, but his wife seemed okay. She said she saw it, too, and he's seen it before. They live down here."

"Might be worth asking around about it," Autumn said. "Leave the tracks there and see if anyone else comments."

"I was planning to do that," Zach said. "Did you get my texts last night?"

"Yes." She got quiet for a minute. "This goatman that you saw at the campground sounds different from other cryptids you've investigated."

"How so?"

"If you're right about it speaking to you at Shadow Point, that makes it intelligent and aware of what you're saying. It could be learning to communicate with humans by mimicking sounds. Maybe that's how it draws people close to it. And it attacked you. It's aware that humans could pose a threat to it."

Zach thought about that. "Maybe." He explained about Elizabeth's notebook and their conversation last night. "She's kept good records. Hopefully I can look through it again today or tonight."

"Sounds like you're keeping busy."

"I do wish you were here. How's the conference?"

"The two-day class starts today, then the main exhibition hall opens tomorrow night. We're on a break, but people are heading back into the room. Let me know if anything big comes up."

"Bye, Autumn. Love you."

"Love you, too," she responded. Zach smiled. Breakfast would be ready by now. When he looked at the schedule, he saw that the winery gates would open at noon for visitors and vendors to set up. The first band would start playing at three this afternoon.

Zach sorted through the brochures and closed his eyes. The one that landed on top would be the winery he'd visit today. He opened his eyes and took in the name Legends Vineyard. Elizabeth had mentioned it last night. He set the brochure aside without looking through it and left the cabin in search of food.

When he reached the tasting room, he discovered that his hunch had been right. Other than himself, only the winery staff had served themselves and were seated both inside and out on the patio. Zach gathered his food and found a table on the edge of the patio, already grateful for the umbrellas that provided shade.

"Hi, Zach," Nancy greeted him. "Mind if I join you?"

"Go ahead," he replied. She sat down in the chair across from him, placed a coffee mug on the table, looked around, and sighed.

"It's going to be busy here over the next few days," she said. "We have almost one hundred people in tents and RVs that will be setting up in the fields down there. Four bands playing each day, starting early afternoon for two-hour sets. We serve breakfast and dinner as options, but guests are on their own for lunch and snacks. It's a great time."

"Is it this busy at other wineries?"

"Yep. Grape Valley also has people camping, although they do have the advantage of having their tavern on the property. Mariah and Morgan always feature jazz musicians, mostly soloists or small groups. Over at Legends, Bob and Anna do have some camping space, but most of the action the next few days will be tourists coming to hear the storytellers and a couple of bands."

She listed a few other wineries and their attractions. "What are your plans for the day, Zach?"

"I thought I'd head over to Legends around noon, then come back here to catch some of the music."

"No problem. You'll find that you'll have some neighbors down at the cabins when you get back."

"Someone slept in the cabin next to me last night."

Nancy laughed. "Bob and Anna. Bob likes wine, and sometimes has a little too much when he's away from home. Anna's learned to always carry an overnight bag with them. It doesn't happen often, but sometimes they need to find a place to sleep rather than make her worry about having to get Bob home."

"Doesn't she drive?"

"Yes, of course, but last night she was very tired. I offered them that cabin. Sally will be down there soon to clean it up and get it ready for the weekend guests." She stood and picked up her mug. "I better go chat with some of the employees. Enjoy Legends, Zach."

"Thanks." He finished his breakfast and brought his plate to an empty bin, then walked back to the cabin. After a couple of hours of reading, then watching a video online of a supposed lake monster in Crater Lake, he left the cabin and locked the door. It was time to see what waited for him at Legends Vineyard.

CHAPTER 10

The minute that Zach saw the entrance to Legends, he knew why Elizabeth had kept quiet about what he'd see there. An eight-foot-tall fake hairy ape, with a goofy smile and a large wine glass in his hand, pointed the way into the parking lot. It was busy, and Zach managed to find a space at the end of a row. He made sure the vehicle was locked and joined the crowd heading for the tasting room and gift shop.

"Maybe I should have actually looked at the brochure," he muttered to himself as he stopped to take a few pictures of the statues surrounding a large courtyard. The Jersey Devil, a lake monster, Bigfoot, a dogman (or werewolf, as the sign called it), and other creatures greeted the winery customers. He headed for the tasting room, not surprised to see a similar layout to the one at Old Forest. This room was twice as large, though, and more staff were behind the counter. He also saw a large footprint cast mounted on a shelf over a wine display featuring bottles with Bigfoot on the label.

Zach studied the board on the wall that advertised wines and prices. He was not much of a wine expert, and he doubted most of the people here were, either. They probably knew whether or not they liked white or red wine, or something in between, and relied on the staff here to guide them into trying new flavors and vintages. He decided to try something here and maybe buy a couple of bottles to bring back to Autumn.

As he waited for his turn to be served, he saw a woman enter the room through an open back door that led to a patio. He immediately recognized her as the woman who had stayed in the cabin next to him last night. She disappeared into a room behind the counter. She emerged again with a man, and Zach nodded as he realized this was her husband. They wore jeans and shirts with the Legends logo, and he realized they worked here.

The man said something to his wife and turned to go back into the room. He saw Zach and touched his wife on the back and said something to her. She turned her head and stared at him, then gave a small smile and a wave. Zach smiled and waved in return.

When Zach reached the counter, he asked the server what she recommended. She explained that he could order a tasting flight of four red or four white wines, and then gave him a sheet listing the available types. He ordered a white wine flight, and a cheese plate to go with it, then took a small sign with a number and a picture of the Jersey Devil on it and brought it over to an empty table out on the patio.

He was joined just moments later by the man. "I guess you figured it out," he said. He offered his hand. "Bob Ryan. My wife, Anna, and I own this place."

Zach was surprised, but tried to not to show it as he shook Bob's hand. "You're the owners?"

Bob sat down. "Yep. Nancy invited us and the Grape Valley owners over so we could go over all of our individual plans for the weekend. It's always nice to know what everyone's doing. We all compete for sales, even if it's a friendly competition on weekends like this."

"There were three other people there. Who were they?"

Bob shrugged. "Winery owners beyond Vineville. We have close ties to Old Forest Cellars and Grape Valley because we share the forest as a boundary between us. Other places in the region have their own characteristic landmarks."

Anna brought Zach his wine and food on a tray. "I see you've officially met," she said. "I'm Anna Ryan." Zach shook her hand as well.

"I know you're busy," he said, looking around. "Let me ask you one question. Did you really see Bigfoot last night?"

"No," Bob admitted. "And in answer to your next question, we planted those footprints at the cabin."

"What did you use?" Zach asked. He was disappointed, but had to admit to himself that there was also some relief. A possible deadly dogman and shadow people were enough for to worry about. Adding Bigfoot to the list of creatures to look out for would have been almost too much.

"A plaster cast we bought from a friend who found a footprint up near Mount Rainier," Anna said. "He made some copies and gave us three of them for the vineyard. One is hanging up in the gift shop, and one is in the tasting room. The other is always in the truck."

"How often have you done this?"

"Only a few times," Bob said. "The first time was over at another winery, after the former owner refused to participate in the art and music festival. I went over during the night and left one print near his car. I hear he was raving about a Bigfoot being around for days." He chuckled. "Then we did it to a couple of people that we know. And you, of course, last night."

"Once Bob recognized you, he thought it would be fun," Anna said. "Nancy mentioned you were down here to do research for a book."

"Yes, I am." Zach smiled. "Mind if I add this story to a possible chapter on hoaxes?"

"Not at all," Bob said. He grew serious. "But there have been stories about Bigfoot down here for a long time. Some people also claim they've seen something that looks like a humanoid goat, and also a werewolf type of creature. Is that what you're here for?"

"I honestly wasn't sure what I'd find when I came down here," Zach said. "Have you actually seen Bigfoot?"

"I think so, though I can't be too sure," Bob admitted. "I was walking in Old Forest one day last summer and could hear branches cracking along the trail. When I stopped walking, I heard a loud grunting sound and then a heavy rock flew past me, over the trail."

"We've read enough Bigfoot encounters to know what that means," Anna added.

"I caught a glimpse of a large, hairy arm before I hurried out of there," Bob said. "Have you asked the Old Forest staff about their encounters?"

"I've spoken to Damon and Elizabeth," Zach replied.

"Well, I'm sure Nancy and her staff are telling you all that they know," Anna said. "There have been strange happenings at the place for years."

She looked around. "Oh, goodness. I better get back to work. Bob, why don't you explain the wines to Zach?"

Zach received more information on wine in the next twenty minutes than he had learned in his entire life. He tasted each small glass, then circled the items he enjoyed in the pamphlet. Bob eventually left to attend to other business, and Zach stood up from the table. Someone came over right away to clear it for the next customer, so he headed over to the gift shop.

He studied the footprint cast hanging above the register. It was the first thing he noticed as he entered the shop. He browsed around the shop, intrigued by the vast array of items. There were a lot of wine-related souvenirs and Oregon calendars and shirts. He found a t-shirt he liked with the Legends Bigfoot on it, then wandered over to the wine section and found two bottles. Both varieties had been in his wine flight earlier. One of the bottles featured Bigfoot. The other one simply had an empty forest clearing pictured on the front with suggested shadows hanging around in the background.

He paid for his items and left, then slowed down on his walk back to the truck. There were people waiting for spots and a line of cars waiting in the long driveway. He wondered if Old Forest was already this busy. Legends certainly had a touristy feel to it, so maybe people were drawn in by that. Zach had noticed that statues of Bigfoot seemed to draw attention no matter where they were placed.

He put the bags in the truck and followed a path, located beside a statue of what appeared to be the Loch Ness monster. It led down to a creek, a continuation of the one he had seen at Grape Valley last night. No one else had come down here yet, so he lingered for a few moments and looked around. It was a quiet and peaceful grotto, with some benches beside the creek. He sat down on one and something in the water caught his eye.

Intellectually, he knew that this creek was too small for a creature the size of most lake monsters. However, just around the bend of the creek, before the water disappeared from sight, he thought he saw a neck extending from the water, with a head that had two large eyes trained on Zach. Just as soon as he caught a glance of it, the creature sank back into the water.

Zach blinked his eyes and waited. Sure enough, ten minutes later the neck and head emerged again. Zach walked along the creek for a couple of minutes and looked down into a fenced area near a group of ferns. He found a mechanical device that appeared to be connected to something in the water. He waited. The device started making noises, and the creature disappeared again.

He smiled. Bob and Anna were giving their guests exactly what they expected to see. He decided to check out a few of the other paths. He exited the lake monster grotto and found the path that had a snarling Bigfoot standing at the entrance. This led back to a different section of the creek. Several people were sitting on rocks under the shade of a few trees and talking loudly to each other.

Zach ignored them and stared across the water at the fence. He walked a few feet to his right and saw a large gap in the links. He was not the only person to see the outline of a hairy figure moving beyond the gap and along the water. One of the women sitting nearby gasped and grabbed one of her friends.

"There's something over there," she said. Her friends just laughed. She looked over at Zach. "Did you see it?" she asked. "It was tall with brown fur."

Zach was troubled by what he had glimpsed this time. The timing was almost too perfect, and something about the action of whatever creature was out there seemed natural. He frowned and nodded, then walked away before the woman could say anything else. He wondered if it was just the power of suggestion from the statues and pictures here, or if he had just caught a glimpse of another Bigfoot.

He left the path and found the tasting room again. The woman and her friends had followed him and sat down at a table. "I saw Bigfoot!" the woman said loudly, drawing the attention of several other customers. Anna, who was walking by, stopped to chat with the woman. Bob also approached the table and said something to the group. When he turned, Zach noticed that he seemed to be trying to hide a smile.

"What's going on here?" he wondered out loud as he located another path, this one heralded by the infamous dogman. It was again labeled as a werewolf at the base of the statue. He followed it and noticed that instead of ending at the water, he came out onto yet another patio with a small outdoor bar. The creek was not visible, but the Ryans had built a wood fence around the chain link one to preserve the aesthetics of this outdoor dining area.

Signs on the fence warned of monsters beyond in the woods. The Legends staff serving food and drink scurried back and forth, seemingly unconcerned about anything that might be in the forest. Just as Zach was about to turn away, he heard a loud growling sound. The customers stopped talking. A howling sound followed, then a large wolf paw appeared over the fence, scratched it, and retreated back into the forest.

"Just another mechanical thing this time," he assured himself. The customers didn't seem worried as service resumed. In fact, some of them were laughing, and one older man turned to his wife. "I told you that would happen," he said, and they both laughed.

Zach decided to try one more path. This time, he chose the Mothman statue. The path led to a deck that overlooked the vineyard. Trees were thick on both side of the deck, making the guests focus on what was in front of them. Zach was alone again, and he turned just in time to see a pair of large, glowing red eyes glaring at him from the forest. They disappeared by seeming to fly up to the top of the trees. He waited, and was rewarded with seeing another Mothman on the other side. He didn't bother to look for the mechanism being used this time.

Zach retreated back to the parking lot and realized that the other paths probably all led to similar areas, either for relaxation or dining. There was nothing more to see here, but he wondered how long the Ryans could keep fooling people before they became numb to the possibility of real monsters.

He drove away, heading back to Old Forest. Along the road, he stopped a couple of times to check out some movement in the fields. Even in broad daylight, there were areas along the roads here that felt creepy. If someone broke down along the highway during a different time of year, it might take a long time for help to arrive. Not days, because the area was much more populated than a person might think. But in the hour or two that a tow truck might need to find a car, Zach guessed that any creature waiting out there would have a chance to observe or attack a human.

As if conjured by his thoughts, he saw a car pulled over on the side of the road, close to a slightly open gate attached to a chain-link fence. He pulled over and got out, but didn't see anyone around. The gate had a no-trespassing sign, and he was not surprised to see that the land belonged to Legends Vineyard.

"Hello?" he called out. He walked around the car and saw that the keys were in the ignition. "Not very smart," he said, and tried the door. It opened, and heat from the car sitting in the sun wafted out at him.

He saw nothing inside that bothered him. There were some music discs in a soft black holder and a t-shirt on the front passenger seat. He decided to not look in the glove compartment and wondered if the driver was still close to the road.

He backed away and closed the door. The gate was already open, so he decided to go through it. Before he set out into the patch of forest, he retrieved his backpack, put on his thin jacket for extra protection from the bushes, and made sure the bear spray was in his pocket. He locked the truck and entered the gate.

This seemed like a forgotten corner of the vineyard, and it was obvious that there were no grapes growing in this patch of land. "Is anyone here? Do you need help?" he called out. He saw something move between a couple of trees a few hundred feet away.

Here I go again, he thought, and moved forward to investigate what seemed to be a large creature observing him.

CHAPTER 11

He found his phone and turned on the camera function, then took some pictures of the trees. He walked forward, feeling confident that he would find nothing. When he reached the place where he had seen the creature looking at him, there was indeed nothing there. He took more pictures of the foliage around him on the chance that something was hiding and the camera would catch it.

He felt the hair on his neck stand up. Something was watching him. Zach heard a wheezing sound behind him. He turned around and was surprised to see the head of an ape peeking at him from behind a tree just a few feet away. It was a little over six feet tall, with dark eye sockets that appeared almost empty, and it seemed intent on letting Zach know it was there.

Zach brought up his phone, keeping an eye on the creature. He was starting to wish that he had brought one of the head-mounted cameras he sometimes used on the show. He took a step forward and the Bigfoot stayed still. "Hi," Zach said in a quiet voice as he started recording the encounter.

The creature moved back behind the tree and walked through the brush. The forest fell silent. Zach walked over to the tree and filmed the few footprints that he could see. They seemed closer together than prints he had previously found after Bigfoot encounters. He was kneeling down to check for signs of hair left behind when he heard the wheezing sound again.

He stood and turned around. This time he was able to see the full body and register that something looked wrong about the creature when it swung a branch covered with leaves. It hit Zach in the stomach and he stumbled backward into several ferns.

He realized that the branch was from a small tree and that he was not hurt. The Bigfoot seemed to want him to leave rather than hurt or kill him. He fumbled in his pocket until he felt the canister of bear spray.

The creature took a step closer to him, and Zach saw that its eyes, at first seeming to be dark sockets, were instead very human. Realizing what was going on, Zach's anger got him off the ground. He pulled out the spray and pressed the trigger, forcing the mist across the ape-like face.

"Fuck! God damn!" he heard. The Bigfoot dropped the branch and stumbled around the trees. Zach followed it, studying the costume that had almost fooled him.

"Sit down," he ordered calmly. He guided the person to a log and removed the Bigfoot head to reveal a tall heavyset man. His breathing was accelerated, either from the spray or from the poor costume ventilation, causing the wheezing noise Zach had heard.

"What the hell?" the guy asked. Although the mask had taken the brunt of the spray, the man had tears running down his face and his nose was running. "What did you do to me?"

"Bear spray. It's pretty much like pepper spray," Zach said. He took off his pack and reached for water, a towel, and tissues. "I know we're still somewhere on Legends property."

"Yeah. Bob and Anna hired me to wander around on this side of the creek and try to get people's attention, then run away. The guests notice an arm or think they get a glimpse of a large ape face and start spreading the word about seeing a Bigfoot here."

"You weren't worried someone might shoot at you?" Zach let the guy dab at his eyes and nose. "What's your name?"

"Jake. Jake Ryan. Bob's my uncle."

Zach looked up the number for Legends and asked to speak to Bob. Jake held his head still and poured water over his eyes, then coughed a few times. Bob finally came on the line. "Hi, Zach! How are you?"

"I'm here in the woods behind your vineyard with your nephew, Jake."

Bob was silent for almost a full minute. "Oh."

"He came at me with a branch. I'm guessing that was just

to scare me out of here. I responded with bear spray. I don't think there's any damage, but you should come down and get him to a hospital or clinic to check him out."

"We're awfully busy. Can you take him?"

Zach looked at Jake. He was still angry, but knew that Jake should get some medical attention. "Okay, but I'll leave him at the hospital. He'll call you when he's done." He ended the call. "My truck is just outside the fence, next to your car. I can almost see it from here. Can you walk?"

"I think so, if you guide me." Jake blinked his eyes. "Good, I can still see. I don't think I should drive, though."

Zach helped him up. Jake tucked the hairy head under his arm. "Have you done this before?" Zach asked. Jake seemed to be having trouble with the large feet on the costume.

"A couple of times. It was better in December, because that costume gets really warm."

"Anyone see you?"

"Yep. I mostly stay across the creek from the tasting room. There are some nice shady spots there. I can sit and get up now and then and look out from the trees. Anna told me two people reported seeing a Bigfoot yesterday."

They reached the truck. "Can you help me take this off? I don't want to wear this to a hospital."

"Sure." Zach located a couple of garbage bags and helped Jake out of the suit. He took some pictures of it, including Jake holding the head and smiling despite his red eyes and nose. Jake was wearing a tank top, shorts, and sneakers under the hairy outfit.

Zach drove into Albany and left Jake at the hospital. There were a couple of smaller urgent care clinics along the way, including right in the center of Vineville, but Zach felt like making Bob drive out of his way. He watched Jake walk into the emergency room, garbage bags in hand, then drove back to Old Forest. At some point during the ride, he relaxed and even laughed for a couple of minutes. He shouldn't have been surprised that Bob and Anna would try to draw attention to their winery by faking Bigfoot sightings when they had already confessed to faking the prints outside his cabin.

As he again thought about including a chapter on hoaxes in the book, he passed the line of cars going into Old Forest and turned down the road leading to the cabins. He parked the truck and waved at Damon, who was walking up the vineyard road with an older, dark-skinned man. "Looks busy over there," Zach said, gesturing to the tasting room.

"Yep. We were just taking a walk down the road to make sure people weren't hanging out in the vineyards." Damon turned to the other man. "Uncle Marcus, this is Zach Larson. He's here this weekend doing research for a book on monsters, like Bigfoot."

"I've seen your show a couple of times," Marcus said. "Nice to meet you, Zach."

"You too, Marcus. I hate to ask right after meeting you, but have you seen anything you can't explain?"

"Thought I saw a dog walking on two legs through the vineyard last October. It was during a full moon, a harvest moon, and I figured it was a prank." Marcus spoke into the radio he was carrying with him. "But Damon keeps insisting it was real."

"Elizabeth was telling me that you had looked into the disappearances of several people in the past few years."

"Yes." Marcus looked at Damon. "It happens. People come through Albany and think the whole area around it is a few minutes from any help they might need. Then they reach places like Vineville and walk off into the fields and forests, get lost with no cell service, and succumb to the elements or get attacked by wild animals."

"There have been sightings of wolf-like monsters around here during the festivals," Damon added, speaking to Marcus.

"Call it what it is. A dogman," Marcus replied. Zach smiled at the shocked look on Damon's face. "I think it's a coincidence. Some of those missing people may have encountered one in the woods, but I think it's been around here for awhile and more people are looking for them now."

"I hadn't considered that," Zach admitted. It made sense. With the popularity of shows like *Creature Hunt*, people had started to be more open about going out and looking for cryptids. Autumn was a member of a small group that had been going on hunts for proof of Bigfoot for several years. It was possible that some of the dogman sightings around the winery were the result of such excursions.

"I better get back up to the patio and pavilion," Marcus said. "I'm sure I'll be seeing you again, Zach. Nice meeting you."

"Same here." Zach shook his hand and Marcus walked up the path, disappearing around the corner of the tasting room.

"Did you see anything interesting today?" Damon asked.

Zach pulled up the pictures of Jake. "Check this out."

Damon laughed. "What happened here?"

Zach explained the story of the Bigfoot tracks near his cabin and his sighting Jake at Legends. "It's people like this, like Bob and Anna, that cast doubt on the efforts of people trying to do real research."

Damon nodded. "I knew about the Ryans sometimes leaving fake tracks. Hiring someone to play Bigfoot is new." His eyes focused behind Zach, and Zach turned around. Elizabeth was at the top of the path, waving.

"I better get back to work, too," Damon said. He jogged up the path and he and Elizabeth walked out of sight.

Zach closed the truck door. He glanced at the ground behind the cabin and frowned. Something wasn't right. He walked over and looked down. There were several, large, uneven footprints leading away from his cabin, into the trees.

Zach backed away, feeling overwhelmed. Bob and Anna had been busy all day. The tracks they had made were still visible on the other side of the cabin. He took pictures of everything, then turned and looked at the vineyard. He saw nothing among the rows of grapes, but still felt a shiver go down his spine.

He retrieved his items from the truck and retreated into the cabin, relishing the cool air. He was glad that Anna and

Bob had been quick to admit their responsibility when he had challenged them about the prints and the Bigfoot hoax. He wished all people who deliberately left false casts, or rented gorilla costumes to get supposed footage of Bigfoot, would be just as honest.

Zach picked out a few snacks and placed them in his backpack. He made sure his wallet, cabin key, and phone were in the bag. He locked the cabin door, waving to some of the other guests now occupying the cabins around him, and headed to the pavilion. He hoped to hear some good music and enjoy himself for the rest of the afternoon.

CHAPTER 12

Zach stayed away from his cabin until after dinner. He mingled with people, talked to some of them about the show, and enjoyed the bands. He ate dinner with Nancy and Damon when they were able to take a break. When Elizabeth was finally able to get away from the tasting room, the last band of the night had just started playing.

"I made those copies for you," she told him as she stopped by his table on the way to the office. "Do you want to look them over again?"

"Sure." He followed her and was amazed at how quiet the building was once he was inside. When Elizabeth shut the front door, he could barely hear anything except for the clock at the end of the hallway.

"It's so quiet in here," he said.

She nodded. "When Nancy realized that both she and I were going to be living here full time, she put some money into making sure that when the winery gets noisy, we'll be able to sleep. Even after the band finishes late at night, people will be getting ready for bed and going back to their tents, sometimes sitting outside and chatting."

Zach nodded. "That was thoughtful of her."

"It also means, though, that when I sit up and wait to see if monsters appear, I can't hear anything unless I go outside or open a window. I've done both."

"I'll probably go back to the cabin soon. Maybe if the rest of my neighbors stay up here, I can go out to the vineyard and start looking for something."

"Check on that with Nancy," Elizabeth advised. She handed Zach a bound copy of all her notes. "She might be able to tell you where to go."

"Did Damon tell you what happened at Legends today?"

"No," she said, looking intrigued. "What happened?"

"I actually caught someone in a hoax," he said. He described Jake's costume to her, and his use of the bear spray. "Hopefully he and Bob learned a lesson."

"I wouldn't count on it," she said. "Bob is determined to have people believe that monsters roam the land over there. Watch out when you're down in the fields later."

"I will," he promised. "Thanks, Elizabeth." He placed the binder in his backpack. He left the office and walked back out into the warm evening. The pavilion was lit with bright strings of white and blue lights, and people were dancing to good cover versions of rock and country songs. Zach walked around the perimeter of the lot and could hear crickets chirping and a light wind blowing through the fields of grape vines off to his left.

He paused, suddenly feeling as if something was watching him. He turned around. Elizabeth was nowhere in sight. Some people on the patio looked his way, but then focused on themselves or their friends and family again. He took a few more steps, unable to shake that feeling. It was still with him as he entered the tasting room.

Nancy and Damon were wiping down the counters. A few other staff members had opened up an outside bar just before dinner, so the room had closed down at its regular time. "I'm heading off to the cabin," Zach told them. "Would it be possible to take my truck down into the vineyard?"

Nancy nodded. Damon grabbed a map and opened it on the counter for Zach. "This is your cabin," he said, circling the small building. "The end of the field just beyond it is our eastern border. If you get back on the gravel road that brought you to the cabins, you can keep driving until you see several other roads that branch off from that one. They go through the vineyard. The gravel road eventually ends at the edge of the forest here. There's a fence with a lot of signs on it. The gate should be locked."

"You'll also see signs on each road that tell you only winery staff is allowed," Nancy said. "We don't have security people patrolling down there, but even the staff here who haven't met you know you're here this weekend and were told that you could go anywhere you wanted. Just let them know who you are if you run into someone. They will be wearing an Old Forest shirt."

"Thanks."

"If you're going exploring down there, I'd suggest only using your parking lights and leaving when no one else is around. We don't want a lot of other people to get the same idea," she added.

"I agree." Zach took the map. "Thanks. I'll see you in the morning."

"Hope so, man," Damon replied with a grin.

Zach walked down the hillside, following the path back to the cabins. About halfway down, he started to hear footsteps behind him. He turned, but couldn't see anyone. As soon as he stopped, the sounds stopped. He started walking again, and after a few paces he could hear the bushes on the side of the trail moving. Something was following him.

He stayed calm until he saw his truck. He broke into a run, twisted open the canopy window, jumped inside, and pulled it shut behind him. He huddled on the bed of the truck, glad that the windows were all still covered with curtains.

The truck rocked as something hit it hard enough to move the equipment chests. He smelled the faint odor of rotting animals. Something brushed against the side of the truck. Zach stayed low as he slid over to the weapons stash and pulled out another can of bear spray and a knife. He made his way to the back window again, where he could hear something moving around on the gravel outside.

He pushed the curtain aside slightly, hoping for a peek of the dogman, or whatever else waited for him. He saw a tall, hairy body just outside of his line of sight, but wasn't able to see it clearly. It was thinner than a Bigfoot would be, and seemed to sense that Zach was trying to look at it.

He heard the creature moving away and looked out again, this time pushing the whole curtain aside. The area around him was quiet. He climbed out of the truck bed with the bear spray and knife, then placed them into the backpack. He had almost forgotten that he was wearing it. He checked the back of the truck and saw a small dent near the brake light, along with a scratch on the tailgate stretching from the window down to the brake light.

He unlocked the cabin door and closed it behind him, then dropped his bag and sat down in a chair. The smell of the dogman, which was what Zach presumed he had just seen, was almost the same as he had noticed when he had seen Bigfoot and previous dogmen. This creature had been eating other animals in the area, and Zach realized that the dogman had no problem stalking and playing with its prey before a final attack.

Zach was now determined to see if he could find out where the dogman was living. It was the first time he had done this on his own in a long time. Even when he had first sent his audition tape to the producers of *Creature Hunt*, there had been a friend with him to help with camera work and pilot the boat while Zach had gone looking for a lake monster.

He remembered that, and shuddered. He could handle almost any creature that walked, crawled, or flew. He did not like the idea of monsters underwater, where they could stay hidden until they wanted to be seen. When they had explored Lake Champlain and other watery areas for the show, Zach had kept his anxiety about such creatures to himself. It was one of the few things that he didn't like hearing about or exploring. He didn't even like to swim in lakes, rivers, or oceans. He preferred to be in pools, where he could see the bottom.

He took a deep breath, then got ready to go out. He changed his clothes, putting on black jeans and a short-sleeved black shirt. He folded a jacket into his backpack, attached the bear spray and the knife to pockets on each side where he could easily get at them, then used the bathroom and splashed water on his face. He emptied the pack of all remaining food, replaced it with a bottle of water, and left the cabin.

After checking to make sure no one was watching him, human or otherwise, he got into his truck and started it. This was a perfect time to go looking for monsters. He backed his truck out of its spot and turned down the road. In his rearview mirror, he thought he saw something run across the road from the field to the cabins. He braked, but nothing moved. *Probably a squirrel or raccoon*, he told himself, and laughed. Neither of those creatures would be mistaken for the black shape he had seen.

He backed up and looked again at the cabins. This time he saw a tall shadow next to his cabin. It appeared to be the same one he had encountered at Grape Valley last night. It stayed still and seemed willing to wait for Zach to make the next move. Zach felt the same sense of being watched that Damon had described, despite seeing no eyes on the creature.

The shadow person suddenly moved. Zach had difficulty finding it again, because this time it didn't set off the motion sensors. He watched it dash across the road with very human-looking legs, and it disappeared back into the field. He shook his head and swore, then realized that the shadow person had probably been sent to keep him here and away from the exploring the vineyards and forest. He took his foot off the brake and started down the road again.

CHAPTER 13

Zach drove quietly down the gravel road, jostling a few times when he hit small bumps. Far away from the lights of the winery, the fields down here were dark and menacing. He heeded Nancy's advice to keep his headlights off. Once or twice, he stopped for small animals, but nothing else jumped out at him.

He saw the end of the road. It was marked with a chain-link fence. He pulled his truck up against the fence, making sure to place the passenger side against the structure so he could easily get back in when he returned. He grabbed his flashlight, placed his backpack on his body, and climbed out of the truck. He quietly shut the door behind him, leaving it unlocked. The keys were in his front jacket pocket, and he made sure the pocket was zipped tight.

He checked the fence and found a gate leading out into the forest. There was a chain and a padlock, but the lock was open and the chain was easy to move. He hesitated before opening the gate. He hadn't gone into the vineyard yet, and those vines could be a good hiding place for an animal stalking its prey. He turned around and decided to walk back down the road until he found one of the paths into the vineyards.

He only walked one hundred yards before he found a sign that warned trespassers away and stated the only access was for winery employees. He stepped off the gravel road and into the grape vines. He turned his flashlight off and stood still, looking around him and up at the sky.

He marveled at how clear the stars were out here. In the distance, he could see the lights from the pavilion, but he knew no one would hear him if he called for help. Thinking about needing help, he checked his other pocket. His cell phone was there, although quick check showed a weak signal.

The rows of vines themselves were not as high as Zach had been expecting. The supports they were growing on were about five feet high, and he could see over them. In fact, he could see well enough in the darkness to make out the shadowy figure that now stood at the end of the row he had just entered.

"Hello?" Zach called out softly. He held the flashlight and turned it on, keeping it pointed at the ground.

"Hi," a soft and familiar voice answered. Zach knew it wasn't the creature who had been stalking him earlier. He slowly brought the light up and pointed it at the figure.

"Elizabeth," he said in relief. "What are you doing here? And how did you get down here without me seeing you?"

She smiled. "Electric golf cart. I know the road pretty well and the stars were enough to see the ground. I also saw your flashlight as you headed down this way."

"I wasn't expecting to see anyone," Zach said, joining her. "Did you happen to go past the cabins?"

"Yes. I felt like I was being watched, but I didn't see any lights on or anyone standing at the windows."

Zach nodded. "Okay."

"Are you out here to see if you can find any cryptids?" she asked.

"Yep. I was going to head out past the fence into the woods back there. I want to know where the dogman has found shelter."

Elizabeth shook her head. "I'm not sure that's a good idea. If the dogman is here, we've already established that this is its prime hunting spot."

"I'm still going down there," Zach insisted.

"Want some company?" she offered.

Zach shook his head. "I'd rather just worry about myself right now."

"Does your girlfriend go on investigations with you?"

"A couple of times," Zach said. "But we know how each of us will react to something. I've never been in those woods before, and I'd prefer to get it a sense of it myself."

Elizabeth nodded. "Okay. Do you mind if I wait for you while you go in there?"

"Actually, I'd appreciate that," he told her.

"Okay." She drove him back to the fence on the cart and stopped behind his truck.

"This looks different," Zach said. He pointed to the gate. "That was still closed when I left it. Now it's open."

Elizabeth stared at the gate, seeming to be lost in her own world. "Do you know what's in those trees?" he asked Elizabeth.

She shrugged. "Just the forest." She gestured to a wooded piece of land on the winery side of the fence. "I think there are some clearings in that area where the seasonal workers go to hang out after quitting time."

Zach touched his knife to reassure himself. He had the feeling that anything he met in there would be beyond the use of bear spray. "Thanks, Elizabeth."

"You know what? I think I'm going to head back," she said suddenly once he was halfway to the fence. "I'll see you tomorrow." With no further explanation, she turned the cart around and sped back up the road.

What the hell is that about? Zach thought. She had been eager to accompany him here, then to stay here and wait for him. It was as if something had really spooked her.

He walked through the open fence. The darkness seemed to be pulling at him. He had only felt this way in one other situation. The television crew had been looking into the legend of the Pope Lick monster in Kentucky. They had gotten close to the train trestle where the monster supposedly lurked, and Zach had felt something low and dark calling to him. Almost trance-like, he had gone beyond the established barrier and started walking over to the trestle. Brandon had seen him and pulled him back, jolting him back to reality.

He felt almost that same sense of displacement now. He turned off his flashlight and tucked it into a loop on his pack. He used both hands to move bushes and trees aside as he entered the forest and seemed to be engulfed by a cool, light mist that waited within the trees.

He found a small clearing and sat down on a log, his back

to a large tree. He felt calmer than he thought he should be, but something out there seemed to want him to be here. He looked across the clearing and saw a tall figure in the mist.

It was standing on two legs, with one arm leaning against the trunk of the tree, as if it was casually waiting for him to notice it. A large hand reached up to a healthy-looking tree limb and bent it down. The creature put up its other arm and in one swift move tore the limb, nearly six inches across, directly from the tree trunk.

Zach was jolted back to reality and realized that he needed to be on guard in this forest. He removed the knife from his pocket and held it up in front of him. Bob's footprint casts might have been a joke, but this was the real thing. Bigfoot did exist down here.

He wondered if this creature and the dogman competed with each other for food and resources. Autumn had once asked him if he thought two types of cryptids could exist in the same place. He was excited that he could possibly answer that question now. His heart was racing, but he managed to slide his phone out of his pocket, hold it low, aim it in the direction of the monster, and take a few pictures.

The creature stared at him and growled. Zach felt that growl deep in his bones. Suddenly, the spell was broken and the Bigfoot turned and ran off into the woods. The log Zach was sitting vibrated from the footsteps. Once again, he smelled rotting flesh and winced. He hoped that was from the Bigfoot and that he hadn't sat down near a rotting deer or raccoon.

Zach realized he was sitting in the dark, on a log, with only the light from his phone screen and some shaky pictures to let him know that he had not been alone here. He took a few deep breaths. His encounter left with him with more questions, and he needed to get back to his cabin so he could start answering them.

Debbie drained her glass of wine and winced as the band started another song. "I'm done," she said to her friends.

"What?" Steve asked. He had been drinking since mid-afternoon. She was glad that Mark's aunt had reserved one of the cabins here for the four of them.

Tina gave her a sympathetic look. "You want to go back to the cabin? I'll go with you."

Debbie shook her head. "I want some time by myself."

Steve shook his head. "Come on, babe. The band's only on its second song."

"I know," she said sharply. Seeing the surprise on Steve's face, she relented and smiled. "I'm not in the mood for music right now. I'll see you when you're done here."

Steve stood and kissed her, then dropped back down into his chair next to Mark. Tina squeezed her arm. "You sure?"

"Yep." Debbie picked up her wine glass and placed it in Tina's bag. She set out across the pavilion lawn. Having only drank one glass, she was alert and able to walk steadily around the pond. A couple of people were out on the dock, and Debbie was tempted to go sit there for a few minutes.

The cabin was waiting, though, and so was her bed and the book she had started at the hotel yesterday. She would be glad to have walls around her. It would be better than the tent they had almost slept in the other night.

She passed though the patio and left the party behind her. She started down the hill and walked quickly down the path. She was almost at the cabin when she looked straight ahead and her heart nearly stopped.

Debbie saw an animal hunched on the ground in the middle of the road. It appeared to be a wolf. Something was strange about its eyes. They were glowing, and the mouth had long fangs hanging out over its lips.

She stared at it. She had seen wolves before, but this one was larger than any other she had seen. Its eyes remained on her even as she walked a few steps to the side. It seemed to be talking to her, telling her that it would not hurt her if she wanted to come closer and touch it.

As she watched, the wolf walked to the vineyard behind the cabins. Debbie, still under its spell, decided to follow it.

The wolf turned and glanced back, as if making sure that she had seen it. She got to the road and the wolf suddenly disappeared into the grapes.

She came out of her trance and realized she was in the middle of the road. She turned and saw vines shaking a few rows away. "Hello?" she whispered, aware that no one else was around. Lights were on in the cabin closest to the road, but she heard no noise coming from inside.

She walked down the road, not sure how far she was going or how much time had passed. When she reached an area of shaking vines, the wolf stepped out into the road again. This time it seemed to be grinning at her. She smiled back, but the smile turned into a silent scream as the wolf rose on its hind legs. She heard the creaking of its bones as her mind raced to explain what she was seeing in front of her.

She screamed. The wolf, or whatever it was, growled and she noticed its large paws. Finger-like claws reached out for her. She turned to run and felt one of the claws scrape against her back. The wolf's jaw snapped behind her.

She was suddenly blinded by headlights and a horn. The wolf growled and ran off into the vineyard. Debbie was shaking, and she felt a human arm steady her. "It's okay," a comforting female voice said. "My name is Elizabeth. I work here."

"What was that?" Debbie asked as she started crying. "First that goat thing. Now a werewolf?"

Elizabeth tightened her grip and led Debbie to an electric-powered cart. "Where are you staying?"

"Cabin 6."

"Okay, good. Let's get you back there."

Debbie nodded. She would get inside, go straight to bed, and forget about all of this. "Yes, let's go."

Elizabeth drove the cart straight to the cabin. Debbie did not notice the man standing on the porch of Cabin 7, or that Elizabeth nodded to him. She felt in her pocket for they key. "Are you going to be okay by yourself?" Elizabeth asked as she walked Debbie to the porch.

"Yes," Debbie said numbly. She replayed the image of the wolf standing on its hind legs like a human. "It was going to kill me."

"You're safe now," Elizabeth assured her.

Debbie went inside and forcefully shut the door behind her. She splashed her face with water, calmed herself down with some chocolate, and sat up in bed, staring at the window. She was sure that the creature was going to be back to find her.

"Where does the dogman live?" Zach asked himself as he typed the words into a document on his laptop. "Why does it make more appearances when more people are here?"

He found his head full of questions. A scream from somewhere in the vineyard pulled him away from the table and he pushed aside the curtain. Seeing nothing, he stepped outside onto the porch. He saw a small cart drive down the road, past the cabins, heading closer to the vineyard. Zach thought he saw Elizabeth behind the wheel. He wondered what she was doing, and stepped off the porch, leaving his door open. He walked over to the road. He saw brake lights in the distance, then they disappeared and it was completely dark again.

It was only a few minutes before Elizabeth returned, this time with another woman in the cart. Zach heard the woman sobbing, and saw that her shirt had a tear in the back. Her face and hair seemed familiar to him, and he wondered if he had seen her someplace else recently. Elizabeth walked the woman up to the cabin closest to him and spoke to her. The woman went inside her cabin, slamming the door with a bang that echoed over to Zach.

Elizabeth walked over to Zach's cabin. "I was doing a check on the gate," she told him. "That woman saw the dogman. She also said something about a 'goat thing' but I don't know where she saw that."

Zach nodded. "I think I saw her and her friends driving into Shadow Point as I was leaving," he said, suddenly seeing that curly blond hair again through the back window. He looked at the car. "Yeah, I recognize the car now."

"I better get back to the tasting room. It's getting late," Elizabeth said. "Good night."

Zach nodded. He closed the door and returned to his work. A little after eleven, he heard voices approaching. He stepped out onto the porch again and saw several people going into the other cabins. Two men and a woman approached Cabin 6.

Zach looked down at the ground and realized that the large prints were still there. He wasn't the only one to notice them. "Hey, Steve," one of the guys called out to his friend, who was just opening the door of the cabin next to Zach. "Look! Bigfoot was here!"

"No way, Mark," the other guy said. The girl that was with them leaned against the doorway, looking like she just wanted to go to sleep. Steve stumbled over to his friend and they both stood silently looking at the prints. Zach looked at the men more closely, and realized that Steve had been driving the car that was going to Shadow Point. Zach smiled, relieved that he and his friends seemed to be okay, then gathered his face into a serious look when the two men glanced over at him.

"Dude, did you see these?" Mark asked.

Zach leaned over the porch railing and looked down. "Whoa! Those are huge!"

"Yeah. Some big hairy ape probably walked through here looking for some grapes," Steve said. He and Mark both laughed, obviously drunk. Zach laughed along with them.

"Come on," Steve said. "I'm buzzed and Debbie's probably already sleep." He waved at Zach. "'Night, dude."

"Good night." He watched them go into the cabin and chuckled. Bob and Anna had probably assumed he would get rid of the tracks. He had almost forgotten about them, but they were still clear enough to attract attention.

He turned and headed back to the cabin. As he passed one of the footprints, he hesitated. A large paw print was visible inside the track. In the light from his window, he could see a couple more indentations in the grass leading around to the back of his cabin.

He looked nervously at the open door. He wondered if he should find someplace else to stay for the night. He could sleep in the truck, but the neighbors might think that was strange.

He ran into the cabin and closed the door. He waited. Nothing was inside, at least not in the main room. He edged over to the bathroom and looked in. Nothing. He turned on the light. Still nothing.

"This is freaking me out," he whispered. He checked the locks on the door twice, then turned on both beside lamps in addition to the overhead light. He sat back down at the table and returned to his notes, looking back at the binder now and then.

Elizabeth had added her sighting to the binder, and when he reached that page he read carefully through her description. The image of a canine hunched over a dead animal was often the first thing people mentioned when they saw the creature. They thought it was just a normal dog or wolf, depending on where they saw it, until it stood up and walked away on two legs. He was starting to think that the creature was hanging out here more for the convenience of water and small animals than for any possible human prey.

He looked up around eleven-thirty and was startled to see two yellow eyes looking in at him through the window across from the table. He stared at them, and recognized the eyes of the dogman. He had looked into those eyes last year, and had seen intelligence and evil at the same time. Now, he wondered if the dogman wanted to make Zach his next victim.

"Not going to happen," Zach whispered. He kept one hand on the table and used the other to slowly draw his camera over to him. He turned it on, and set it upright on the table. Looking down to the screen, he focused on the eyes and snapped three shots. The creature just blinked, then backed away from the window with a growl.

Zach went to the door and listened. All was quiet outside, and he hoped no one else was looking out their windows right now. He armed himself with bear spray, then opened the door. The dogman stood next to a window at the cabin next door. Zach stepped forward and pressed the button to release the spray. The dogman smelled it and ran off into the vineyard. Zach was relieved. Maybe he could finally get some sleep tonight.

CHAPTER 14

When Zach woke up on Friday, he decided that he needed a break from the winery and the creatures and people around it. He looked at a map and realized that Seaport, a town on the coast, was less than two hours away. He made some coffee and got dressed, deciding to pick up breakfast on the road.

By ten o'clock, he was parking in a public lot in Seaport. The ocean crashed against a beach in front of him and he rolled down his window to listen to the surf. He could see a few people already walking on the sand. It was a clear day, but a strong breeze was keeping the town cooler than the area around Old Forest.

He joined the rest of the tourists in walking down the streets, looking at gift shops, candy stores, and ice cream parlors catering to visitors. Seaport had a small aquarium and Zach was intrigued by a display in the lobby. It was a large, mechanical creature that looked like a prehistoric sea monster. According to the display, the creature had been given the name Porty.

Zach read the story of Porty and noticed that Seaport had a history of strange animal sightings off the coast, as well as some carcasses washing up on the beach. He examined the pictures carefully and looked at what was claimed to be a piece of sea monster skin carefully preserved in glass. He took some notes on his phone, decided to look up the rest after he got home, and put the phone back in his jacket.

He was turning away from the display when the creature's eyes blinked and the head turned to look at him. Zach was startled, and took a couple of steps back. The staff member closest to him chuckled. "Almost looks real when it does that, right?"

"Almost." Zach took a closer look. The display was clear that the animal was fake, but when he touched the skin it felt real. "It's a pretty convincing monster."

He strolled through the rest of the aquarium and smiled at the tanks, impressed by the number of animals they had on display. He didn't mind seeing sea creatures when they were safely behind glass and not able to touch him.

He paid for a small basket of fish to feed to the seals in an enclosed tank, and laughed when one took its snack right from his hand. After washing his hands, he emerged into the bright sunshine and blinked. He was hungry, and it was time for lunch.

He found a nearby restaurant with a Bigfoot statue, carved from wood, just outside the front door. He took a picture, then asked the hostess to take a picture of him with the statue. She obliged, then seated him in a quiet corner.

He looked around while trying to study the menu. The restaurant did have a Bigfoot theme, but it wasn't overdone. The ambience of the dining area was focused on the customers feeling like they were dining in a forest with the comforts of being inside a log cabin. As he ate his lunch, he overheard some conversations and was relieved that they were about the other people's plans for the day, not about Bigfoot sightings.

When he left the restaurant, the beach across the street seemed to call out to him. He bought some ice cream and sat down on a bench overlooking the ocean. He watched the waves closely, his mind trained by now to look for unusual things. For a brief moment, he thought he saw humps that could be a large sea serpent, but they jumped out of the water and he realized it was several seals following each other.

He walked on the beach for an hour, then returned to a gift shop and found a sweatshirt for Autumn as well as one for himself. He lingered in Seaport until the late afternoon, enjoying the scenery and people watching. When he passed by the aquarium again, he couldn't resist going in and having another look at the sea creature.

This time, the aquarium manager was standing by the display. "Hi, I'm Larry Owen," he said. "I think I saw you earlier today on our cameras."

Zach looked up in the corner and saw the security camera. "Zach Larson."

"I knew you looked familiar. What do you think of our sea monster?"

"The signs say it's fake."

"This one is, yes. But it's modeled after one that was found on the beach in the early twentieth century. I have pictures of that and some skin samples if you'd like to have a closer look."

"I would like that," Zach answered honestly. He followed Larry into a long hallway. The manager opened a door marked "Staff only" and led Zach down another hallway to an unmarked door painted in red. They entered a dimly lit room, and Larry turned on the overhead lights and pointed to a work bench with three stools.

"Have a seat. I'll get it from the drawer."

Zach sat down and looked at the pictures on the wall. Someone had taken a lot of care in preserving the local history of underwater monster sightings. Some pictures, obviously taken by tourists, showed the typical sea serpent heads that had taken hold in the public eye. Some photos were labeled as being from lakes throughout the state.

Larry returned to the bench with a box and carefully set it down. He removed some marked containers and Zach picked one up to examine it. A rotting, scaly piece of flesh sat inside, and he opened the lid. He didn't touch it, but did take pictures.

"How long has this been back here?" he asked Larry, looking around for something to write on.

Larry handed him a small pad of paper and a pen. "I was told that it's been back here since the creature was found. As you can see, it wasn't well preserved. The man who managed this place before me finally did what he could with the samples. We keep them back here, in cold storage, and only take them out for people like who you are doing research or have a serious interest."

Zach nodded and took notes on the condition of the skin. He looked at the other containers, which held several teeth, a piece of skin, and what looked like it might be an eye. The eye was huge, and Zach shivered. "Imagine being out there in the ocean and suddenly this creature swims past you," he muttered as he finally put the camera away. "I'd panic just from seeing those eyes, let alone those teeth."

Larry nodded as he gathered the specimen containers back into the box. "We really tried to duplicate that effect when Porty was built."

"The creature out in the lobby? You helped make that?"

"I was young, just starting out as a marine biologist." Larry returned the box to the storage area and sat down next to Zach. "The people who ran this place were looking for something to draw people in. At that time, Porty was outside. It didn't take us long to figure out that we either needed to cover him up or put him inside the aquarium. The manager added signs outside advertising Porty, and it worked. Once people were inside, it was easy enough to get them to pay to see the rest of the aquarium."

"Which is quite an attraction in itself," Zach said. "I went through the whole place earlier."

Larry looked up at the clock. "We're about to close. Did you get what you needed?"

"Yes. I'm working on a book about cryptids in the Pacific Northwest. Porty will be a good addition."

"I look forward to reading it when it's finished."

"Thank you for your time."

Zach shook Larry's hand, then walked back out into the lobby. He lingered for a just a couple more minutes to look at Porty, amused at the name but realizing that it fit the town. He certainly had more than enough new photos and notes to add to the chapter on underwater monsters.

He realized it was time to return to the winery and get some work done. He stopped to get fast food for dinner, and found the road leading to Old Forest around seven o'clock. He passed the public areas, filled with people dancing and talking while a rock band played on the pavilion stage. He passed a line of cars waiting to park and reached his cabin, grateful to be off the road.

He brought his souvenirs into the cabin and brewed more coffee. The minute he had parked outside, he had once again felt like he was being watched. He stepped out onto the porch and saw a shadow person crouched down among the vines. Even though it was still dusk, it was a sold black color and he could see it sway, as if its position was uncomfortable. As he watched, it seemed to melt away into the ground.

He drew back inside and sat down to look at his computer. He wrote several pages about the goatman, trying to get himself caught up while the event was still fresh in his mind. He finally got tired of typing and moved over to the bed to lay down. It was only a few minutes after eight, and he promised himself he'd get a quick nap and head over to the tasting room before it closed at ten. He shut his eyes and immediately had visions of the goatman coming after him again, the blade of its weapon gleaming brightly in firelight.

CHAPTER 15

Zach woke up to a knock on his door and groaned. "Just a minute," he called out. He pulled on a sweatshirt and walked over to the door, opening it slowly.

Bob Ryan nearly shoved him down as he entered. "Close it, close it!" he said in an urgent tone. He was carrying a tote bag with the Old Forest Cellars logo. Zach closed the door and reached for the light switch.

"No, don't let it know we're here!"

Zach, now fully alert, was instantly annoyed. "Bob, what the hell is going on? If something is out there, it probably already saw you come in the door."

There was enough light coming in through the window that Zach saw fear on Bob's face. "There's some sort of dog-like monster following me."

"Are you sure it's not someone in a werewolf costume?"

"Are you serious?"

"Yes. You have a variety of tricks going on. Is this a ruse to get me outside where you'll have people waiting to get me on camera falling for a hoax?"

"Look, I understand why you'd think that. But I swear, something is stalking me out there. It's on two legs, has yellow eyes, and when it turned its head, I saw a profile like a dog." Bob sat down at the table. "I've seen it before, in the fields near Legends. In fact, I saw it just as we were leaving to come over here. I saw it here when we arrived. Somehow, this thing knew where I was going and followed me. I can't imagine how fast it must have been running, but it was waiting in the trees when I parked my truck."

Zach pulled all the curtains shut after looking out the windows and seeing no monsters watching the cabin. He turned on the bedside lamp. "So why come to me, Bob?"

"You're the monster hunter. Can't you make it go away?"

"I'm here to document sightings. I'm not out to capture anything, except on camera or video. I'm not here to kill anything, unless it attacks me."

"What if this thing has already killed?" Bob rested his face in his hands. "It's scary, Zach. I've never felt that something was really evil until this thing looked in my direction. I swear, it was grinning at me, telling me it was going to come for me soon."

Zach remembered his dogman encounters in Minnesota. He had felt the same way that Bob was feeling now. "There are a lot of dogman sightings down here, Bob. It will probably go away for a time, and then someone else will see it later."

"So, what am I supposed to do?"

Zach shrugged. "I guess what everyone else does. Watch your surroundings and try to not give it a chance to get you alone in the forest." He sat down across from Bob. "Why did you come here tonight?"

"I found something. Anna and I were at the pavilion enjoying the music, and I was getting restless. I decided to take a walk down in the vineyard." Bob shook his head. "Bad idea. I was at the end of the road, down by that gate, and almost tripped over this." He reached into his bag and pulled out a skeletal paw.

Zach gently took it from him and placed it on the table. "Wait. You just happened to have an Old Forest bag with you?"

"I found a couple of them on the ground down there, like someone dropped them. The paw was near a tree."

"Which side of the fence?"

Bob hesitated. "Not the winery side. At the base of a tree in Old Forest."

Zach recalled Elizabeth driving down to the gate last night. She might have had a couple of bags on the cart with the rest of the supplies that were carried around the winery. He turned back to the paw. The bone was hard, and the fingers that extended from the base were long. The bones were yellow, and Zach guessed that they had once been buried. He was amazed that it was still in one piece. "Do you know what this means?"

"Someone buried a dog or wolf out there."

"No. There's more than one dogman out there."

He ran his hand over the paw. He had no experience in trying to date bones and wasn't an expert in canine biology. He would have bet anything, though, that this paw wasn't new. It did have some damage. There was a crack in the side that could have been from an injury. If it had been inflicted while the creature was alive, the dogman could have been in a lot of pain and unable to walk or hunt.

"Oh, don't say that." Bob's voice was tense.

"Maybe you should go back to the pavilion," Zach suggested. "I'd like to look at this for a bit longer."

"Walk with me," Bob begged. Zach could see fear in the older man's eyes.

"You know what? Sure. I could use some fresh air. Just give me a few minutes."

"Okay." Bob disappeared into the bathroom. Zach took pictures of the paw and saved them on the laptop. He then placed the paw carefully in his own backpack and slid it over his shoulders.

Bob returned to the room, and Zach handed him the tote bag, now only holding a blanket and a couple bottles of water. Seeing the contents, Zach realized that Bob had lied about finding the bag on the ground, and had probably brought it with him in hopes of finding some sort of new display for his winery. "Let's go," Zach said. He opened the door and motioned for Bob to leave, then followed him and locked the door.

They could hear a band playing country music. No one else was around, and Zach could not see anything lurking under nearby trees except for a glimpse of one of the shadow people. Bob didn't seem to see it, so Zach didn't point it out. He sensed it watching them, though, and knew it was probably following as they walked up the short hill. He stayed behind Bob, who said more than once that he was comforted by Zach's presence.

They reached the patio and Bob sighed. "Thanks, Zach.

Have a good night." He ran in the direction of the pavilion to rejoin his wife.

Zach peeked into the tasting room. To his surprise, it was nearly empty. The patio and pavilion were busy, but only Nancy, Damon, and Elizabeth were seated at a table inside. Marcus stood near them, listening to Nancy as she advised him about the final events of the weekend.

Elizabeth saw him first. "Zach! How are you? I haven't seen you all day."

"I'm good, thanks. I was out at the coast, in Seaport, for most of the day. I got back here a couple of hours ago and I just had an interesting visit from Bob Ryan."

Damon groaned. "What's he up to now?"

Zach pulled the paw out of his bag and placed it in front of them. Elizabeth gasped. Nancy stared at it. Marcus and Damon moved closer to look at the bones. "He handed this to me," Zach said. "On first glance, it looks like it could come from a dog. Or a wolf. Or a dogman."

Marcus smiled grimly and shook his head. "Dogman bones? I mean, I believe there's a creature stalking around the forest out there, but why would there be visible bones sitting around? You'd think scavengers would take care of a dead body."

"That's one of the usual theories about why cryptid remains aren't found," Zach agreed.

Elizabeth remained quiet. She ran a hand over the paw. "Where did he find it?" she asked, not meeting Zach's eyes.

"Down by a tree at the back of the winery. On the other side of the fence, so he was probably out there hoping to find something in the forest." He looked at Marcus. "He's most likely been sneaking around back there for some time. I think he saw something on a previous trip, maybe signs of a Bigfoot, and wants a piece of the monster to take back to Legends."

Nancy studied Elizabeth's demeanor. "Elizabeth? Is there something you're not telling us?"

Elizabeth nodded and bit her lip. She looked at Zach, her

eyes moist. "I found this a couple of years ago."

"Where have you been keeping it?" Nancy asked. "I've never seen this in your office."

"Let me guess," Damon said. He reached out to comfort Elizabeth by putting his hand on her arm. "In that shed down by the back gate."

"Most of the time," Elizabeth said. "That's where I first stored it. Last December I brought it up to the office and kept it in a drawer under a towel. It was the drawer where I always keep personal supplies, so it was locked."

"Maybe the dogman is looking for it," Marcus said. He felt the paw and winced as he ran his hand over the long fingers. "These probably ended in sharp claws. If this creature attacked, it would probably easily kill its victim."

"I tried to bring it back last night," Elizabeth said. "I unlocked the gate and saw a truck heading my way. I hid the cart and waited until Zach walked into the vineyard, then slipped outside the fence and placed the paw under a tree. When I returned to the fence with Zach, I was shocked to find that I had forgotten to close the gates." She blinked. "I should have left it out there when I first saw it. Maybe the dogman got mad and started going after people."

She cried. Everyone sat in silence for a couple of minutes. Zach finally spoke, wondering if he was really prepared for what he was proposing to do. "I think you should return this to where you found it. Tonight."

Elizabeth nodded. Nancy sighed. Marcus and Damon both touched the paw, then also nodded in agreement. "I'll go with you," Zach offered.

A knock sounded on the door. Another Old Forest employee stuck her head inside the room. "Nancy? People are asking about buying some wine."

"Okay. Let them in." Nancy stood and headed for the counter. "Damon, can you stay here and help me?"

"Sure," he said, looking disappointed. He shook it off and smiled. "Good luck."

Marcus backed away from the table. "I need to check in

on my team."

"Looks like it's just us," Zach said to Elizabeth. He saw the fear in her eyes as he returned the paw to his bag just as some people entered the tasting room. "It'll be as quick as we can make it. Let's take a cart down to the gate, put the bones back, and leave."

"It's stalking me," she whispered. "I saw it behind the house earlier today. In broad daylight."

"Let's get it away from here," Zach whispered back.

Elizabeth nodded. She and Zach left the room and found a cart parked behind the building. "The missing people aren't your fault," Zach told her as she drove the vehicle down the hill and passed the cabins. "This dogman, or dogmen, have probably been around here for a long time. You taking the bones might have focused some attention on you, though."

"It knows I have the paw. How can it be so smart?"

"It probably saw you take it and recognized a scent or something else about you. I can only assume they have the same traits as most canines."

"Do you think this will end its visits here?"

"I don't know," Zach answered honestly.

They turned onto the road through the vineyards. Zach kept his eyes wandering across the rows of grapes and thought he saw something large running between the vines on four legs. He knew that he had the bear spray and his knife, and hoped he wouldn't need them. Elizabeth kept her eyes focused on the road. They pulled up to the gate and saw that it had once again been unlocked and was wide open. Both of them saw what was lurking just outside the forest beyond the fence.

CHAPTER 16

"The dogman is waiting for us," Elizabeth said. "I could swear I saw it back by the cabins when we drove down here."

"It can move fast."

They left the cart and Zach handed the paw to Elizabeth. "I'll be right beside you," he assured her. He felt his pocket to make sure the camera was there, then followed Elizabeth to the gate.

The dogman, having waited for them in an upright position, dropped to a normal canine stance and headed into the woods. Zach found the bear spray and held it as Elizabeth led him down a path he hadn't noticed before. They were a few hundred feet into their walk when Zach realized his flashlight was still in his backpack. The light from the full moon was bright enough to guide their way.

"Here," Elizabeth whispered. She stopped at a large pile of logs.

"Oh my God," Zach whispered. He had seen a structure like this before, when he had first met Autumn a couple of years ago back in Tahoma Valley. It was an organized pile, with branches clearly torn from trees and arranged to create a shelter. "Bigfoot," Zach said.

"What?" Elizabeth hissed. Zach took pictures as she walked around the shelter. He followed her to a large circle bordered by a variety of stones. "I found it in here," she said.

"Was that shelter here two years ago?"

"Yes. I saw nothing else around here, and it seemed clear that it wasn't occupied by humans at the time. I thought someone had camped down here for a bit, then maybe got chased away by something."

"What made you think that?"

"There were some scattered pieces of clothing inside. A torn flannel shirt, a canvas bag, stuff like that. I thought they had been left behind or found and collected by someone."

"Or something. This wasn't built by humans," Zach said.

"What?"

They heard loud thumps approaching them. A glance at the other side of the circle showed them that the dogman was watching them from behind some bushes. Elizabeth stepped into the circle and the dogman growled. She showed it the paw, and its eyes gleamed brighter as she leaned down and set it down where she had found it.

She backed out of the circle and tripped, falling to the ground. Zach rushed to put the camera away and reached out to help her. She rolled over and pushed herself up. "Ow," she complained. "I hit my side on something."

Zach felt the ground. "Another stone?" he asked, pushing aside dirt and leaves that had fallen over an object set apart from the boundary stones. He sat back as the moonlight revealed the partially decomposed hand of what appeared to be a large ape. Zach guessed it to be almost a foot wide across the palm, with fingers nearly as long. Skin was peeling away from bone, and the hand appeared to have been chewed off of a body, probably by scavengers. Zach looked around and thought he saw part of a foot also sticking out of the ground.

"How can that be?" Elizabeth said, seeing the same thing as Zach. "Is this some sort of cryptid graveyard?"

Zach retrieved his camera, ignoring a growl from the dogman. This was a real piece of evidence. If he could somehow get this out of here, he could take it to a lab and have it analyzed. For a long moment, he contemplated picking up the hand, putting it in his backpack, and running for his life to get out of Old Forest.

He shook his head, but the thought remained. The dogman howled, and Zach jumped. He tried to take a few pictures as the creature stepped into the circle. He exchanged the camera for the bear spray and stood in front of Elizabeth. "We need to get out of here," he said in a firm voice. The dogman's ears twitched, and they all turned, frozen in place.

A bulky dark shape stood next to a tree behind Elizabeth. She screamed and grabbed Zach's arm. He held on to her and started backing away, in the direction of the shelter and the path back to the gate. "Let's go," he said.

The creature emerged, revealing a face that had both animal and human qualities. It had long brown hair all over its body, and hands that started to move back and forth when it saw them. It stood at almost eight feet tall, and Zach made a quick estimate that it had to be almost a thousand pounds of muscle. This was no human in a costume. This was a real Bigfoot.

He could hear Elizabeth crying behind him. "Oh, God. Oh, God. Both of these? Here?"

"Just walk," Zach ordered. He looked again at the Bigfoot hand. He longed to grab it and take it with him. He knew what could happen if he dared to take it, though, and realized that he didn't want any part of this to follow him home. The pictures, if he had gotten clear ones, would have to be enough.

The Bigfoot watched the humans until they reached the path. The dogman snapped his jaw at the Bigfoot, who pounded a tree in response. The Bigfoot started to follow Zach and Elizabeth, as if to make sure they were really leaving. The dogman reached down and caressed the paw that Elizabeth had placed in the circle.

When Zach and Elizabeth were several feet back past the shelter, the Bigfoot stopped and bared its teeth at them. It stood at the entrance to the shelter and suddenly raised its arms and roared. The dogman howled in response.

That was enough for Zach. He let go of Elizabeth. "Run!" he shouted. They hurried down the path as quickly as they could. At some point, Zach felt the bear spray drop from his hand and heard it roll off into the forest. He didn't look back until he and Elizabeth reached the gate, turned around, and slammed it shut.

Elizabeth used her shaking hands to fasten the locks. When she was done, she stumbled to the cart and sat down hard in the passenger seat, her shoulders heaving and arms trembling. Zach settled into the driver's seat and studied the fence. The creatures had stayed behind in the forest, having successfully driven away the humans.

Elizabeth tried to drink some water from the bottle Zach offered her. He had to steady her hand to get the liquid into her mouth. She shuddered, and took a few deep breaths.

"We're okay," Zach assured her. "I think they'll stay away now, if no one else disturbs them."

"Does it always feel like this?" she asked quietly. "When you see them, I mean. I was scared by the dogman. When I could look into its eyes, I felt it wanted me to leave the forest or suffer for being there. I was not expecting to see Bigfoot. The look on its face was almost human, yet there was no doubt it was an animal."

"I found some tracks earlier, that Bob didn't make," Zach admitted. "And I thought I saw a Bigfoot here last night, so I've already discovered that two large and dangerous cryptids are sharing this territory."

"Did you act like this when you first saw a Bigfoot?" she asked. "And don't try to tell me that you haven't actually experienced one in person before now. You're way too calm for that."

"I've had personal encounters with Bigfoot and two dogmen," Zach said.

"Weren't you scared?"

"Nervous. Yes, there was some fear. In the moment, I had to defend myself from the creatures and ended up drawing blood. I wasn't happy about it, but it was necessary. I think that helped me to realize that they're just like other animals, with their own weaknesses."

"I like that thought," Elizabeth said, nodding her head. Her voice was clear again, and she had stopped shaking.

"Ready to go back?"

"Sure."

Elizabeth grabbed her sweatshirt from the back of the cart after realizing that she had somehow ripped her polo shirt in their adventure. They drove past the vineyards, turned at the cabins, and came across Damon and Marcus on the patio just outside of the tasting room.

"How did it go?" Damon asked. Zach saw Bob and Anna standing nearby, talking to Nancy. Bob was trying hard to look like he wasn't interested in what Zach and Elizabeth had done.

"We returned the paw to what looked like some sort of burial ground. There was also a Bigfoot hand," Zach said quietly. He didn't like the look that appeared on Bob's face, but decided that he had other priorities right now. "I'm taking Elizabeth back to the house. She's had a bit of a shock."

Marcus nodded. Zach drove across the patio, avoiding the party that was winding down over at the pavilion. They pulled up in front of the house. Zach guided Elizabeth into her office and closed the door behind them. She sat behind her desk, appearing to have completely calmed down, and he sat across from her.

"Are you going to be okay?" he asked.

"I think so," she said. "Do you think the dogman will stay out of here now?"

"Possibly. The Bigfoot hand concerns me."

"Why?" she asked, her eyes focusing sharply on him.

"It seems to be from a recent death, so the creature we saw will be very protective of it. I think that Bob heard me talk about it. He might try to go out there and find it." Zach thought about the gate. "He might have already been looking for it."

"I'll check on it myself after you leave tomorrow," she promised. "Do you want some coffee?"

"If you're having some."

She brewed two cups in her coffeemaker and handed the mug to him. "It's good," she said as she sipped the warm liquid. "I feel better now."

"Good. You might have some trouble sleeping tonight. That's normal."

She nodded. "I'm not going to add this encounter to our winery sightings book."

"I don't blame you." Zach looked up the pictures from the excursion and shook his head. "It was too dark and I was in a hurry to get out of there. I did get one of the hand, but all I can see is some flesh and a piece of bone. There's no way to tell how big it is. I probably won't be able to use any of these."

"Too bad."

Nancy came in the front door and knocked on the office door. Zach opened it. "The crowd's settling in for the night," she said. "So, what happened?"

Zach let Elizabeth explain, adding a few details when necessary. Nancy absorbed the information with a steady, unchanging expression on her face. "We'll check the gate for a couple of weeks," she agreed. "How are you now, Elizabeth?"

"Good," Elizabeth said. She smiled at both of them. "I guess I have to believe people now when they say they've seen Bigfoot."

Nancy smiled. "It was a busy day. I'm heading upstairs."

"Goodnight," they all said at the same time. Nancy left, and Zach stretched.

"I better get back to my cabin. I'd like to let my girlfriend know what happened."

"I'm sure she'll be excited to hear about it."

Zach thought about Autumn's last Bigfoot encounter. "Maybe. She'll be excited about the paw and hand. She's always hoping for new evidence."

Elizabeth studied her desk for a minute. She reached into her top drawer and held out a key ring with three keys on it. "Before you leave tomorrow, if you decide to go take another look at the hand, these are for the locks on the gate."

He took the keyring. "Are you sure?"

"Yes. Whatever you decide, just give them back to me before you leave. Thanks for being out there with me, Zach. I never could have done it by myself. Not at night, and certainly not without freaking out and probably getting lost in the forest."

"If you go out there again, ask Damon or someone else you trust to go with you."

"I will," she promised.

Zach left the house and walked across the winery. He didn't feel anything watching him, not even a shadow person, until he returned to his cabin. His heart sank as he realized the two men in black suits had found him. It appeared to be the same two people, and he wondered how long they had been looking for him. They were waiting at their car, parked behind his truck. "You found the graveyard?" one of them asked.

"Yes. I'm guessing you're government agents looking for the same things I am."

"What gave it away?" the other one said. His partner glared at him.

"Your expression when we encountered the goatman," Zach said. "You were way too shocked to have already known what you'd experience. You've probably been investigating down here for a year, hoping to see the goatman and somehow debunk it. You recognized me and realized I was probably looking for Bigfoot, so you figured out where I was staying and learned what you could about Old Forest."

"That's a lot of guessing," one of the agents said. "But I won't tell you you're wrong."

"You can stop following me. I'm going home tomorrow."

"Planning a stop at Shadow Point?"

"No, but I'll be back at the Saint Helens Campground. Maybe I'll see a Batsquatch this time."

"Don't joke about that," one of them warned. "You might not sleep for a week if you catch a glimpse of it."

"You should keep an eye on Bob Ryan, owner of Legends Vineyard. I think he's got an eye on the Bigfoot hand."

"Already on it." They backed away, got into their car, and left.

"See you later," Zach muttered. He went into his cabin, relieved to finally be alone and behind a locked door. He turned on a light and closed all the curtains.

After an hour of talking to Autumn, who had been asleep but was clearly wide awake by the end of their chat, Zach turned off the light and stared up at the ceiling. He had a lot to write about, and was happy with most of what he had accomplished on this trip. He hated to walk away from an important discovery like the hand, but trying to take it from here would have disastrous effects.

He decided that he would go back out to the shelter tomorrow morning and document it properly. He'd get pictures of the remains, then leave and let the cryptids live in peace down here. He assumed that they had somehow worked out a way to share the food and water resources, and although it would be interesting to study that, he was not the right person to do it. Satisfied with his decision, he was able to finally fall asleep.

CHAPTER 17

Bob Ryan drove his truck down to the back gate at Old Forest Cellars. He had told Anna that he couldn't sleep and was going over to the office to get some paperwork done. She had simply nodded and gone back to sleep. Instead of the office, he had gone out to the garage and taken out the small sedan they used for non-business trips. It wasn't much use around the winery, but the engine was quiet and it was helpful to have it when he didn't want Anna to know he was leaving the property in the middle of the night.

He had borrowed the gate keys from Elizabeth's office last year and made copies. He had done the same at Grape Valley. Hunting for Bigfoot stuff was one of his hobbies, and he had long suspected that the creature actually was living somewhere down here.

Finding that dogman paw had been a surprise, one that Bob didn't like. That eerie creature had stalked him all the way down the road to Zach's cabin, and he was glad to be rid of it. Overhearing Zach talk about the Bigfoot hand tonight had convinced him to come back and try to find it. It would be a priceless addition to his collection.

He looked around. The winery had been quiet and mostly dark when he had passed along the fence, and all the cabins were dark. He planned to go straight to the trail he had noticed when he was down here last year. He had been chased away by something large and stealthy back then. This time, he would not leave until he either had the hand or was convinced that it didn't actually exist.

He opened the gate and walked into the forest. The moon was bright and he could see the path clearly, but he also used his flashlight. He played the light over the ground to the side of the path now and then. He was startled when something metal reflected back at him.

He reached into the bushes and pulled out a can of bear spray. "I wonder who dropped this," he whispered. He placed it in the tote bag he had removed from the car. It was the one

one he had carried the paw in earlier that evening.

He stopped at the sight of the shelter. This was something he had only heard about in books and shows like *Creature Hunt*. He pointed the flashlight at the entrance and thought he saw something move inside. He turned off the light and stepped off the trail, hiding behind a large tree to assess his options.

The hand should be around here somewhere, he reasoned. He could stay off-trail and keep walking through the bushes to the clearing that was visible about fifty feet away. The only other choice was to stay on the path and walk as quietly as possible around the shelter to get to that same clearing.

He decided to go on the path, as there were more chances for him to get away by taking that route. He stepped around the tree again and saw nothing in front of him, and nothing near the shelter. He carefully walked around it, using the moonlight to guide his way.

He saw the circle of stones. The dogman paw rested in the dirt on the far side of the circle. He wasn't touching that again. He didn't want that monster anywhere near him.

Just a few feet away, Bob saw the large hand of what looked like an ape. He almost shouted with joy, but managed to restrain himself. He opened the bag and picked up the Bigfoot hand. It was starting to rot, and he felt disgusted by the sensation of touching it. He almost dropped it into the bag, but he made himself take the time to wrap it up. He rolled it into a blanket and placed gently into the bag, then backed away from the stones.

He walked back around the side of the shelter, adrenaline rushing through him. His heart beat faster when he saw the Bigfoot at the entrance, watching him. He held the bag tightly at his side and his breath caught at finally seeing the creature with his own eyes.

He had been a fool to hire Jake to portray this beast. Although the ruse might have worked from a distance, Zach had noticed something different about it quite quickly. Bob didn't know if Zach had ever actually seen Bigfoot in person, but it was larger and more menacing than Bob had ever imagined. The images all around the winery didn't do it justice.

In the moment that the two beings stood and studied each other, Bob noticed its hands and face. Long fingers were clenching and releasing, and it looked almost like it was grinning. Bob tried to smile in response.

The creature turned its face up to the sky and roared. It picked up a large stick and approached Bob. When it was just a few feet away, it struck a nearby tree three times with the stick. The sound reverberated through Bob's head, and spurred him into action.

He brought out the can of bear spray. He heard a howling noise from somewhere beyond the clearing. He thought the dogman might be coming, and that was enough for him. He was not going to engage in a battle he couldn't survive.

He released the spray as the Bigfoot lunged for him. The spray covered its face and hairy head with a light mist. The Bigfoot roared and dropped the stick. It started wiping at its face with its hands, its fingers uselessly trying to get rid of the burning pain caused by the spray. Bob seized the moment and ran away.

He reached the gate and looked around to see if he had been followed. He saw nothing, and shut the gate quietly behind him. The hand was still in the bag, feeling hairy and rough when he stroked it. He locked the gate, started the car, and drove back to Legends.

He hurried into the empty and dark tasting room, only turning on a couple of dim lights in case Anna woke up and looked out to see if he was in the office. He got a stepstool and placed the hand on a shelf above the Bigfoot wine display. He realized that the smell of decomposing flesh might be too strong, and found a glass display case for the hand. People would ask about it tomorrow. He'd have to come up with a good story, including one for Anna.

He relaxed against the counter. The hand was his. He could sleep restfully now. He turned off the light and walked over to his house. Along the way, he caught something moving out of the corner of his eye.

He turned and looked at the garage. He saw nothing at first. Then, his eyes fell on the dark figure standing next to the building. It didn't move, and he couldn't see a face, but he still felt as if it was watching him.

"Go away," he whispered. The figure stayed still. Bob turned and for the first time noticed a black sedan parked outside the tasting room. He thought he saw two people inside. He shook his head and ran into the house. "Everything will be okay in the morning," he told himself as he locked the door behind him.

When he climbed back into bed, Anna stirred. "What took you so long?" she asked.

"A package came today that I forgot to open. Someone who was here last year sent what they claim is a rotting Bigfoot hand. It's probably fake, but looks cool. I put it out for display."

"Okay," she said. Bob waited until he thought he was asleep again, then ran through his made-up story in his head. Yes, it sounded good. He could already see the excitement in people's eyes tomorrow at the idea of seeing a hand from a Bigfoot. It would be a great day for Legends.

CHAPTER 18

Zach woke up on Saturday and packed his bags. He brought everything out to the truck. The group in Cabin 6 was just heading along the path up to the patio for breakfast. The blonde woman he had seen the other night turned and looked at him, but did not stop walking.

He had something to do before he ate breakfast. He made sure all of his belongings were out of the cabin, then shut the door and took the key with him. He drove down to the gate and used the keys from Elizabeth to open it.

Zach brought his backpack and knife with him. He longer had the bear spray, so he hoped he wouldn't have to get close enough to an animal to be able to use the knife. He had no intention of physically challenging either of the creatures he had seen last night.

He found the path and walked at a quick pace. When he reached the shelter, he heard an unfamiliar noise. He looked around the structure and was shocked to see the Bigfoot, kneeling by the stone circle, rocking back and forth and moaning.

Zach backed up, trying to not make any noise even though he was sure the creature could sense he was there. He focused his camera and zoomed in on the area where the creature was sitting. The foot had been tucked back into the ground. The Bigfoot hand appeared to be missing.

"Oh, no," he whispered. The Bigfoot ignored him. Although he could only see a part of its head and face, he noticed that the skin around the face appeared to be irritated. A shiny substance coated part of the hair on top of its head. He looked down and saw a bear spray can. He picked it up and shook it. It seemed to be empty. That explained the physical pain of the Bigfoot.

He quickly got pictures of the scene and the shelter. He backed away and hurried down the path. He had a feeling that Bob had come down here and taken the hand. He thought that once the Bigfoot recovered, Bob would be getting an unwelcome visitor.

He locked the gate behind him, thinking about the fact that seeing this Bigfoot did not fill him with the same shock as the first time he had seen the elusive creature. Perhaps it was because it had seemed to be in pain and upset over the loss of the remains. Those behaviors made it seem more human, but Zach knew he shouldn't let his guard down. Given its size, the creature could come tearing out here any minute and do some real damage.

He drove his truck to the front parking lot, which still had plenty of spots available. A lot of the overnight campers were having breakfast at their tents, or down in the RV parking area. Zach knocked on the office building door, then opened it and placed the cabin and gate keys on Elizabeth's desk. He walked over to the patio and found Elizabeth and Nancy eating at a table overlooking the pavilion.

"Hey, Zach!" Nancy waved. "Are you leaving today?"

"Yes. I left the keys in the office."

"Great. Go get some food and join us!"

Zach visited the buffet and selected his food. He included a cinnamon roll, which was Autumn's favorite pastry. He missed her this morning and was looking forward to seeing her again tomorrow. He returned to the table with his food and beverages. Nancy sipped some coffee while Elizabeth played around with a tea bag in a mug.

"Did you get what you were looking for here?" Nancy asked.

"Yes, I did. I hope I wasn't too much of an intrusion."

"Not at all. I was happy to help you, and let my staff help you."

"Anything new this morning?" Elizabeth asked, placing the tea bag on the plate and drinking from the mug.

"I think Bob came back last night and snuck into the forest," Zach said. "He might have decided to take something important."

"Another body part?" Nancy asked.

"Yes. I'm sure you'll be hearing something about it from

any of your guests who go over to Legends today."

"Okay," Nancy said. "Looks like someone in the tasting room needs my help." She stood and shook Zach's hand. "I look forward to reading your book."

"Thanks." Nancy rushed off, and Damon stepped over to the table.

"I hear you're leaving. Come back sometime and maybe I'll have more monster stories for you. Nice meeting you."

"You, too." They shook hands, and Damon followed Nancy to the tasting room.

"I think there's someone you should speak to before you leave," Elizabeth said.

"Who?"

"The woman I saved from the dogman the other night. She and her friends already ate breakfast. The others went over to Grape Valley, but she's down on the dock."

Zach turned and saw the woman with her feet in the water. "What's her name?"

"Debbie."

"Okay." He finished eating and stood. "Come with me."

"Are you sure?"

"Yes. She might be more comfortable if you're there."

They walked over to the pond. Zach followed Elizabeth onto the dock, noticing how murky the pond water looked even in daylight. He would definitely not be putting any part of his body in the water.

"Hi, Debbie," Elizabeth said. Debbie turned and looked at them with a nervous smile. Zach had seen the same expression on numerous witnesses he had spoken to for the show. "This is Zach Larson. He'd like to ask you some questions about last night, if you're up to talking about it."

"You were at Shadow Point," Debbie said to Zach.

"Yes. I was leaving as you were driving in."

"We should have followed you right away," she said sadly. "We wouldn't have seen that goat monster."

Zach sat down next to her. Elizabeth sat on the other side, taking off her shoes and putting her own feet in the water. He looked into Debbie's eyes. "What did you see?"

Debbie recounted the story. Zach was amazed at the similarities to his own experience. He was also still surprised that people continued to stay at Shadow Point. "I encountered the goatman, too," he said when she had finished with their arrival at the hotel.

"Goatman," she echoed. "Yes, that's a good name for it. I've never seen anything like it."

"Most people who have seen it don't like to talk about it."

"I saw your truck at the hotel. We stayed there a couple of nights before coming down here." She sighed. "And then I saw the wolf monster. Does that have a name, too?"

"A few of them. It's often called a dogman, but people refer to it in other ways, too."

"Perfect. I was attacked by a dogman."

"Did it physically hurt you?"

She answered his question by pulling up her shirt. A scratch, bright red, ran from her shoulder to halfway down her back. "It's sore," she said. "And it tore my shirt. I told my friends that I was walking over to see if I could sample some grapes, stumbled, and fell against one of the trellises." She shook her head. "I didn't want Tina to freak out again."

"And the dogman seemed to be luring you down the road."

"Yes. Just like the goatman was trying to get Tina to come over to it." She shook her head. "There's nothing else down here, is there?"

"Have you been over to Legends yet?" Zach asked, keeping his voice light.

"No. We're going there this afternoon."

"People claim they've seen Bigfoot there," he said. "I don't know if I believe that." He laughed softly.

Elizabeth and Debbie laughed, too. "Thanks for listening, Zach," Debbie said. "It's good to know at least a couple of people don't think I'm crazy."

"If you have time later, I'd like to show you a book of other strange things people have experienced here," Elizabeth replied. "You can even add your story."

"I'd like that." Debbie smiled, and this time there was warmth behind it. "Thank you."

"Thank you for speaking with me," Zach said. "Hope the rest of your trip is fun." He waited for Elizabeth to put on her shoes, then they walked to the parking lot.

"She'll be okay," Elizabeth said, as if trying to convince herself.

"I think so, too. She's not going to forget the goatman or the dogman." Zach unlocked his truck. He looked at Elizabeth. "Thank you for everything. I appreciate the help."

She surprised him with a quick, friendly hug. "I'm glad you got to see a few new things, even if one of them was a hoax."

"That happens more often than you might think. Please let me know if you hear any news from over at Legends."

"I will," she promised. "Goodbye, Zach."

"Bye," he said, and smiled as he closed the door. She waved and hurried over to the office building. Zach started the truck, took a moment to decide what route to take back to the Saint Helens Campground, then drove away from Old Forest Cellars.

CHAPTER 19

"That's awesome!" Steve exclaimed as he and Mark posed for a picture in front of the Goatman statue.

Tina frowned, and Debbie sighed while Mariah Dixon took the photo. "I always recommend people come and visit this place while they're down here," she told the young women as Steve and Mark ventured over to the Loch Ness monster statue. "It's certainly got a unique vibe."

"That's one word for it," Tina muttered. Debbie knew Tina was about as happy as she was to be in a place that was devoted to the monsters they had seen this week.

Mariah frowned as she joined Debbie and Tina when they walked over to join Mark and Steve. "We might as well make the best of this," she said. "You already toured Grape Valley and tasted what we have. You're staying at Old Forest. Try to find something good about this place in the next couple of hours," she advised them.

Debbie nodded. "Hey, let's go to the tasting room!" Mark said. "The last time I was down here I wasn't old enough to drink yet and Anna wouldn't let me have anything even with Aunt Mariah here. Now I can see what's so special about their wines."

An hour later, Debbie had to admit she was enjoying herself. Bob and Anna Ryan were well versed in what they served, and Mariah had even been impressed with a couple of their newer wines. Debbie was starting to feel hot and tired, so she suggested they find a place to sit and relax.

"There's a nice shady spot by the creek," Bob advised. "Just follow the Loch Ness monster path."

"Of course," Tina said with a smile. She had consumed the most wine of the group, and Mark had to guide her as they walked down to the sitting area. Mariah stayed behind to discuss some business with Bob and Anna. Steve held Debbie's hand, and she relaxed and snuggled against him as they sat down on a bench under some trees.

They had just all fallen silent when a rock crashed down

onto the cement patio in front of them. "What the hell?" Steve asked. "Why do things keep getting thrown at us?"

A boulder crashed into the water and the resulting splash hit Tina and Mark. Debbie looked at the rock. It was almost two feet across. She couldn't imagine a forest animal having the strength to lift that. She also couldn't imagine a human doing it.

A roar echoed across the creek. Debbie moved away from Steve and saw the gap in the fence. She stopped in a spot right across from it and watched in horror as a large arm tore through the foliage on the other side. A head peeked out from behind a tree, and she realized it was attached to the same body as the arm.

"Oh, shit," she whispered. "He wasn't kidding. Bigfoot is here."

Tina screamed. Mark and Steve looked uncertain of what to do. Steve started to step into the creek, but Debbie shouted at him. "No! That thing will kill you!"

The creature disappeared back into the forest. Mariah and Bob came running down the path, followed by a few other tourists. "What happened?" Mariah asked.

"We saw Bigfoot," Debbie said numbly. "It was across the river. It threw rocks at us."

A howling noise made her gasp. Tina ran to Mark and threw her arms around him. "No need to worry," Bob assured them. "That's coming from the dogman patio."

"I want to see that!" Steve shouted. He and Mark took off running, leaving Debbie and Tina staring at their backs in disbelief. Mariah frowned, but hugged the girls.

"It's okay," she said. "Look, whatever was there is gone."

"Let's wait for the guys up at the gift shop," Debbie suggested. Tina nodded, and they followed Mariah up the path. The other tourists disappeared to different parts of the winery. Bob remained behind and studied the rock that had come to rest on the patio. He knew it hadn't been there this morning.

"Jake!" he called out. He and his nephew had agreed that

they would continue Jake's role as Bigfoot for the remainder of the weekend. Bob had promised that Zach would not come after the younger man again, and Jake had cleaned off the costume. He had gone into the forest again this morning and was supposed to be out there now.

"Jake!" Bob called again, louder this time. He started to become uneasy. He decided he needed to go check on his nephew. He ran back to the house and took the winery truck out to the highway and around to the gate where Jake had parked. His nephew's car was there, unlocked, and it looked like he had put on the costume and gone into the forest.

Bob followed the familiar trail and looked around. "Jake!" he hissed. He didn't want anyone who might be over across the creek to hear him. "Jake!"

There was no answer. He kept walking. Across from the patio, where he could see a couple of guests now sitting, he found the clearing where Jake usually sat. His nephew's cooler bag was there. Half of the ape costume was also there. The head was missing.

Bob looked down and saw blood on the cooler bag. "Jake," he whispered, suddenly frightened and sad. He sat down and waited for twenty minutes, but Jake didn't emerge from the forest. Bob tried calling him, but he didn't answer. Finally, Bob picked up the costume. He left the cooler bag, in case Jake came back, and walked back to the truck.

He had a sick feeling in his stomach. He thought about the Bigfoot hand, the prized object he had been so eager to display in the gift shop. Surely the monster wouldn't be able to find it all the way over here. He waited for a long time, hoping that Jake would come bounding out of the woods with the missing costume piece and demanding that his uncle tell him what had happened to the rest of it.

It was a call from Anna that finally prompted him to go back to the winery. Mariah was going to leave and wanted to ask Bob a few questions. He returned, and Anna could sense that something was wrong, but he managed a smile for Mariah and her guests. The young woman had been correct about seeing a monster.

It was nearly closing time when Bob heard more shouts down by the creek. He rushed down there, and his heart soared as he saw Jake emerge from the gap in the fence. His nephew was bruised and bleeding, but had managed to retrieve his bag. The ape head was torn and filled with branches and leaves, but Bob no longer cared about the costume.

He and Anna guided Jake to the tasting room, where the guests had already cleared out for the evening. "What happened?" Bob demanded. Anna called the paramedics to come and look at Jake.

"I'm not sure," Jake admitted. "I was sitting on the log, and suddenly something grabbed me from behind. I slipped out of the costume, but the head got stuck and I was dragged along the ground for a while. When I was finally dropped, I managed to get the head off and saw a large hairy monster retreating into the forest. I had been shouting, so maybe it realized I was a human and lost interest in me."

Or that you weren't the right human, Bob added silently. "Then what happened?"

"I was dizzy and disoriented. I picked up the head and stumbled around for a long time. I finally found the log and my bag. I don't know where the rest of the costume is."

"I have it," Bob said. "We were worried sick."

Anna hugged him. "Quiet now," she said as the paramedics and a police officer arrived. "You better think of something more plausible than you were attacked by Bigfoot."

Jake was examined, and Bob listened as his nephew made up a story about falling down a hill while hiking. He wasn't sure if the police officer believed Jake, but he didn't care. He was just happy that his nephew was safe. He hoped the Bigfoot would leave Legends alone now and go back into Old Forest, where it and the dogman could live in peace.

CHAPTER 20

On his way back to Washington, Zach decided to make a detour past Shadow Point. It was mid-afternoon when he pulled off to the side of the road across from the entrance. Even in broad daylight, on a summer Saturday, just looking at the driveway into the campground made him shiver. He sat across from the driveway until he noticed a police car pulling up behind him.

The officer approached him, studying the dent in the back of his truck before arriving at the driver's side window. "Can I help you with something, sir?"

"I was here several days ago. I didn't stay the night. Something in there scared me off while I was looking around in that abandoned cabin." Zach realized he was babbling and took a deep breath.

The officer nodded and turned to look at Shadow Point. "We hear stories like that a lot. Had quite a few people in and out of there this week, though, and nothing bad reported to us."

"I called your department on Tuesday and asked them to check on some people who were pulling in as I was leaving. I was concerned, since I thought I saw something that looked like a goat walking on two legs."

"Lots of people have reported that," the officer chuckled. "I've never seen it myself. My partner and I came over here after you called and drove in to the campsites. There were some young adults here, alright, and they were just settling in for the night. We found some alcohol but let them keep it because they were all over twenty-one. When we left, they were sitting around a fire and talking." He shook his head. "We pulled them over a couple of hours later, speeding down the highway. They said they had changed their minds, and we sent them over to the Oregon Inn."

"I saw them at the winery where I was staying," Zach said. "If it's okay with you, I'll be on my home."

"No problem." The officer walked back to his car, and

Zach got back on the highway after one last look at Shadow Point.

After a few more hours of driving, he realized that he was close to the Saint Helens Campground. He stopped for another fast-food dinner, eaten in his truck, and replied to a text from Autumn reminding him of when her flight was due to arrive tomorrow. He got back on the road, and was relieved to see the familiar signs. He was surprised that the place wasn't very busy, especially on a summer weekend, but after the crowds at the winery he thought it would be nice to be around fewer people and hopefully be able to collect his thoughts about the week.

Zach checked in at the counter and waved to Blair, who was on his way out of the building. "Hey, Zach," he greeted him. "How was Oregon?"

Several responses ran through Zach's head. "Busy," he finally said. Blair looked at him and nodded, seeming to understand the message.

"We're actually pretty quiet tonight," the clerk said. "I can give you the tent site close to the bathroom." She used the map to point out the space that Zach had occupied almost a week ago.

"Fine," he agreed. He paid and left the office with Blair right behind him.

"Find anything at Shadow Point?" he asked. "Any sign of what happened to Bill?"

Zach shook his head, then changed his mind and looked right into the other man's eyes. "Do you really want to know?" he asked quietly.

"Yes."

"I looked through the house and found some signs of an intruder and a struggle. While I was there, I had an unsettling experience with something that was hunting me." He cleared his throat, remembering the goatman encounter. "I didn't find any bodies or skeletons, but I would think that Bill is dead. He was probably attacked by that same creature."

Blair looked down at the ground. "I thought that might be

what happened. Thanks, Zach."

"You're welcome. I'm sorry it happened."

"Me, too."

Blair walked over to his house. Zach drove down to the camp site. This time, the nearest RV was six spaces away. He backed in to the site and cleaned up the cab of his truck. He tossed fast food wrappers and empty soda bottles into a bag, then left the truck and dropped the trash in the dumpster. After using the bathroom, he noticed it was almost fully dark. He wanted to crawl into the back of his truck, update his notes, and get to sleep.

An hour later, he was in pajama pants and a t-shirt, looking at his laptop. Someone had already logged on to the BOG forum and claimed to see a Bigfoot near Albany, Oregon, during the weekend. He saw that the post was followed with a bunch of questions from regular members, and a couple of the user names were familiar to him. He didn't see Autumn's name on any recent posts, so he figured she was busy getting ready to fly home.

A loud crack from outside his truck made him jump. His heart raced as he closed the laptop and turned off the overhead light. He reached for his shoes and put them on, then picked up a flashlight and quietly opened the rear window.

He let his eyes adjust and took in his surroundings. The lights along the road barely illuminated the forest line, and at first Zach thought he was imagining the large shape about thirty feet up in the trees just yards from his truck. Branches waved, and Zach heard the cry of an animal that was abruptly cut off. He turned on the flashlight and pointed it up into the trees.

A large, hairy arm was just disappearing back into the foliage. "A Bigfoot. It can't be. That high up?" he said, knowing he was speaking out loud. He shined the light again and red eyes reflected back at him.

Stunned, Zach climbed out of the truck and pushed the button to record a video. "I'm at a campground near Mount

Saint Helens. I just saw what appears to be a Bigfoot in this tree," he narrated. "Could this be the legendary Batsquatch that people claim to have seen around here?"

He zoomed in on the area where he had seen the arm. "It's right there. You can see the eyes." He shined the light again, and this time he heard branches breaking as something descended from the tree.

He dropped the phone and hurried to pick it up. As he looked up again, he saw the red glowing eyes staring at him from the base of a tree. He held the phone steady and waited until whatever the creature was turned and disappeared completely into the trees. He hurried over to see where it had been and found some imprints in the soil that could be from the creature's feet.

Zach realized what he had actually been able to record. He sank down onto the picnic table and started shaking. "No, it can't be real," he repeated a few times. He turned the camera to face him and described exactly what he had seen. He turned it off when he saw other campers approaching his site from somewhere down the road. "Did you hear some limbs falling out there?" one of them called out as they passed his site. "Better be careful."

"Yes, I will," was all he could manage. He forced a smile and waved. They kept walking, and he stumbled back into his truck.

He locked the window behind him and checked to make sure all the curtains were closed. It had been a long time since an encounter had left him so confused. The red eyes and the height of the creature reminded him of stories about Mothman. He had never heard of a Bigfoot climbing high into trees, but realized that they surely had that capability with their long arms and strong bodies.

He played back the footage. He was shocked that, other than the few seconds in which he had dropped the camera, he had actually gotten a clear image of the eyes and the faint footprints. "I can use this," he realized. He connected the phone to the laptop and made copies of the video. He would review it tomorrow.

"Thank you," he whispered to whatever spirit was listening to him. He turned everything off and laid down under a blanket. He kept his eyes open, waiting and listening to see if anything else was out there in the darkness.

CHAPTER 21

Zach woke up later than he had planned on Sunday morning, but a glance at his watch assured him that he had plenty of time. He used the shower and shaved, feeling good when he stepped out into the warm morning air. He returned everything to his truck and took another look back in the forest.

The footprints from last night were gone. Something had walked over them during the night. Zach turned to look in all directions and shrugged. There was nothing to see back here today. He drove to the office, turned in his key, ate breakfast, and said goodbye to Blair and Kathy. When he reached the interstate, he felt like he was leaving the past week behind him.

He was halfway to the airport when he received a call from Elizabeth. "Hey, Elizabeth," Zach said as he answered with his hands-free system.

"Zach, something's happened at Legends."

"What?" Zach asked with a sinking feeling.

"We were right. Bob took the Bigfoot hand."

"How do you know?"

"I got curious and went over there yesterday afternoon. It was already on display in their tasting room. He put it on a shelf up high, next to that footprint cast."

"Oh, no." Zach guessed what Elizabeth was going to say next.

"I guess the Bigfoot can track things down better than the dogman. It tore apart the tasting room and took the hand. It smashed the counter, tossed the barrel tables around, smashed all the bottles, and tossed cases of wine through the windows."

"Was anyone hurt?"

"No, thank goodness. Anna actually left their house to see what was going on, saw a bottle of wine fly out a broken window, and woke up Bob. He called the police. It's mess. I'm standing just outside the crime scene tape right now."

"So, the Bigfoot has the hand again."

"Looks like it." Elizabeth suddenly laughed. "It tried to take its statue along. It ripped it off the base, then maybe lost interest once it realized how bulky it was. It's on the ground near Bob and Anna's house, broken into several pieces."

Zach laughed along with her. "Anything else?"

"They're shut down for at least a week for repairs. Nancy is asking Damon and a couple of other people to help when they can." She lowered her voice. "The police found Jake's costume in the storage room. That caused quite a stir."

"I'll bet."

"Just wanted to keep you updated. So far there's no further sign of the dogman. Marcus is back at work in Albany this week and promised he'd take another look at some of the missing persons cases."

"Good. Maybe other people have turned up and didn't think to report it."

"Let's hope so." Elizabeth turned serious again. "Thanks, Zach. Maybe we'll see you and your girlfriend down here sometime."

"That would be nice," Zach agreed. "Thanks for calling, Elizabeth."

"Bye," she said softly.

"Bye," he replied, and ended the call. He thought about what she had told him as he kept his eyes on the road. Bob had taken the hand and been the victim of a wild animal's rampage. Elizabeth had taken the dogman paw and the creature had stalked her until it was returned. Both body parts had come from the same place, a common graveyard, which still amazed Zach.

He tried to put it all together, but kept coming back to how differently the creatures had reacted. *That works with their size and abilities*, he realized. The dogman was smaller and more capable of stealthy hunting. The Bigfoot was larger and better suited for smashing things.

"Maybe that's why they're able to co-exist there," he said out loud. "They can provide different abilities for survival."

He was excited, and spent the rest of the drive dictating his thoughts to the voice recorder on his phone. He finished just as he pulled up to the curb at the airport and got out of the truck. Autumn was already waiting with her luggage. She saw him and embraced him.

He held on to her for a long time. "How was your trip?" he asked.

"Good. Productive. Yours?"

"Same," he laughed. "But you already know most of it."

"Tell me anyway," she urged as he put her suitcases in the back of the cab and she climbed into the front seat.

He told her everything in the hour it took to get back to their house. She stopped him only long enough to go inside the veterinary office and pick up Squatch. Once she was settled back in her seat, letting the cat rub against her fingers through the carrier door, he finished with a recap of his thoughts on the dogman and Bigfoot sharing the forest.

"Not that they live in the same place," he assured her. "I didn't stay long enough to figure out where the dogman finds shelter. But at some time in the past, they started burying their dead in the same place. It appears that they still do that."

"So, they can co-exist," she agreed. 'That's something for the book. I wonder how many other cryptids are like that?"

"Probably not many. The goatman I encountered didn't seem happy about sharing its space."

"I can't believe you went in that house," she said. "But at least you found a way out."

"I'd do it again," Zach said.

Autumn nodded. "Speaking of doing things again, I think we should go back to Tahoma Valley soon."

"Why?"

"There's a pattern of sightings that are similar to the months before my friends and I went out there a couple of years ago. The BOG forum is all over it. Considering how quiet it's been around there since then, that's a big deal. Maybe the creatures are ready to face humans again."

"Or maybe they'll want some revenge if they somehow

recognize us," Zach said. "I'll think about." He pulled into their driveway. The porch light welcomed them, and the lights they had set on timers shined behind the partially open curtains.

"I'll accept that for now," Autumn said. She retrieved her luggage and brought it to the house. Zach picked up the cat carrier and turned at the sound of a car driving down the street.

He saw a black car and for a moment believed that the two agents had actually followed him home. The window rolled down, and he recognized one of their neighbors. "Welcome back!" the guy said.

"Thanks," Zach replied. The neighbor waved and drove away. Zach walked into the house and set Squatch free. The cat meowed and ran upstairs to join Autumn. Zach walked over to the living room curtains to shut them and saw something dark dash out from behind the truck and disappear through the fence. He frowned.

A shadow person had followed him home. He knew he had not taken anything from the cryptids, so he wondered if this supernatural being was here to make sure of that. He looked at the stairs as Autumn descended, gave one last glance out the windows, and shut the curtains.

They sat down on the couch to look at the pictures Zach had taken on the trip. Autumn was especially intrigued by the pictures of the hand and paw. "Maybe we can find more bones somewhere," she said. She gave him a pointed look.

Zach stayed silent, so she turned back to the camera. As she scrolled through the pictures, he was reminded of the adventure and danger that waited for them if they returned to Tahoma Valley to get proof of Bigfoot. Autumn was ready. Zach realized that he was ready, too.

"Let's go back," he said.

"Yeah?"

"Yes."

She hugged him. He walked out to the truck and retrieved the bottles of wine from Legends, along with the other items he had bought during the week. Cleaning up the rest of the gear could wait until morning. When he returned, she was already on her phone, texting messages to a couple of her friends.

She laughed at the bottle labels. "Oh, those are perfect. Let's have the Bigfoot."

He opened it and poured the wine into two glasses. She set aside her phone and clinked his glass with hers. "So much good evidence now. What are we going to call this book we're writing?"

"I don't know. Something about following a trail of monsters." Zach smiled at Autumn. She nodded. They drank their glasses of wine and settled in to discuss their next investigation.

ABOUT THE AUTHOR

C.E. Osborn grew up in Tacoma, Washington, and currently resides in New Jersey. She is a cataloging librarian and enjoys reading mysteries and stories about cryptid creatures. You can learn more at www.ceosborn.wordpress.com and on Facebook.

Works by C.E. Osborn

Trail of Monsters
Wolf Crossing
October Nights
Creature Hunt
Circle of Darkness
Shadow in the Trees
Camp Thunder Cloud

Poetry:
Dream Softly
Before You Take My Hand

Lonely Hollow series:
Stormy Hollow
Winter Hollow
Lonely Hollow

Printed in Great Britain
by Amazon